SWIFT AND DEADLY RETRIBUTION

The flat voice of the vigilante leader rasped upward.

"You, up there, stranger. You and the nigger boy come out peaceful or we come in unpeaceful. It's your free choice. You get ten minutes."

A horse whinnied loudly into the following silence.

"Ten minutes," the vigilante repeated tonelessly.

After that, only the wind was heard muttering. Ben and the mulatto youth stared at one another. They were trapped.

Two more for the sycamore, sure enough.

OUTCASTS OF CANYON CREEK

OUTCASTS OF CANYON CREEK
CLAY FISHER

A NATIONAL GENERAL COMPANY

OUTCASTS OF CANYON CREEK
A Bantam Book / published December 1972

Library of Congress Cataloging in Publication Data

Allen, Henry Wilson, 1912–
    Outcasts of Canyon Creek.

    I. Title.
[PZ3.A42560u] [PS3551.L393] 813'.5'4 72–8890

Published simultaneously in the United States and Canada

*Bantam Books are published by Bantam Books, Inc., a National
General company. Its trade-mark, consisting of the words "Bantam
Books" and the portrayal of a bantam, is registered in the United
States Patent Office and in other countries. Marca Registrada.
Bantam Books, Inc., 666 Fifth Avenue, New York, N.Y. 10019.*

The Virginia City Stranglers
Rode By Night And Ruled With
The Hangman's Noose—Until They
Put Their Sinister Rope On The
Wrong Man. A Novel Of Big Ben
Allison And The Last Days Of
The Vigilantes Of Montana

"... The administration of the *lex talionis* by self-constituted authority is, undoubtedly, in civilized and settled communities, an outrage on mankind. It is there wholly unnecessary; but ... the question of the propriety of establishing a Vigilance Committee depends upon the answers which ought to be given to the following queries: Is it lawful for citizens to slay robbers and murderers, when they catch them? Or ought they to wait for policemen, where there are none, or put them in penitentiaries not yet erected?"

Thos. J. Dimsdale
VIGILANTES OF MONTANA

OUTCASTS
OF CANYON CREEK

1

The tall man halted his horse in the wintry darkness of the draw. His view looked out into the main canyon, down upon the torches of the hanging posse below. *"Hoh-shuh,"* he murmured to the horse, using the old Indian warning word. The animal flicked ears forward, watching with its rider.

Ben Allison understood that torchlit scene. It was one played out all too often in such lonely rock-walled courtrooms. The vigilantes from the nearby gold camps were at another of their midnight jury trials—putting secret noose to gnarled gallows tree, bringing hempen justice, guilty or not, to the shivering wretch they now would raise to meet his maker, bulging-eyed and frozen in the wind. Damn them! No man should have to die like that, a gunnysack over his head, hands tied behind him. But this one would go that way, for no power could save him now. The Vigilantes of Montana had him.

Ben knew those deadly judges.

It had been but high noon of the previous day that he himself had walked out of Bozeman Courthouse a free man, found innocent of vigilante-brought charges of highway robbery and murder. But a smiling member of the Vigilance Committee had met him on the courthouse steps and told him that, if the next sun found Ben Allison still in Montana Territory, the magpies would eat his eyeballs for breakfast.

Ben had believed the man.

He rode a wide circle to the west, guessing they would be laying for him to the south, expecting him to ride that way for Texas and home. The detour had worked. Just now, leaving Canyon Creek behind, and safely beyond the main Virginia City diggings, he was certain he and the Comanche mustang had "done a true coyote" on the night-riding stranglers. That is, they had played a trick of the trail on them, an Indian trick, and had lost them. It was only blind bad luck that brought them to this dangerous rejoining of their trackline with that of the Vigilantes of Montana.

But now there was nothing for Ben Allison to do other than to turn around and ride away. There was no way to help the poor devil they were hanging. Ben might not even make it free from them himself. Ride out, ride out! his instincts told him, yet something deeper than nature's first law laid a hand upon his shoulder.

An eddy of icy wind prowled up the canyon, flaring the torches of the posse. Ben, turning back to ride out, saw the "Executive," that is, the leader of the vigilantes, reach to pull away the gunnysack from the prisoner's head. He did it to permit the hangman to better fit the ugly three-coiled knot behind the doomed man's ear. But Ben saw only the raggedy-long hair of the youth as it spilled out from beneath the sack, then the fishbelly blanch of the terrified young face and the beardless hollows of the clenched jaws. Jesus God, he thought, that isn't a man they're hanging down there; it's only a boy, fifteen, maybe sixteen years old. What in God's name could a boy have done to deserve the lynching rope?

Ben could not answer his own question, yet something compelled him to *try*. He must know, must find out what was wrong.

He came down off the Indian mustang with the stealth of a six-foot four-inch snowflake. He let the reins fall to ground-trail and the Comanche-trained pony did not move or make a sound. Sliding his Winchester half out of the saddle scabbard, Ben quickly slid it back in again. Surprise and pure gall were the only guns that could get him in and out from under the vigilantes' gallows tree.

He went on foot down out of the side canyon to the

2

main floor, his shadow no more evident than the other shadows. Coming to his objective, a cabin-sized boulder which was gradually edging the gallows tree flat, his pale gray eyes narrowed.

Nothing changed with the vigilantes; they were a human wolfpack. They simply took the trail of their quarry and ran it to its ending in whatever darkened barn or lonely pile of rocks would best muffle the condemned man's cries for mercy or for justice.

Their only law was the ancient *lex talionis,* the law of swift and deadly retribution without open trial.

The accused and his crime were known, his guilt announced in advance. After that, the wolves began to run. When the quarry was trapped, as now, outer guards were posted while the pack finished off the prey. It was the guards which Ben Allison was looking for and, quickly, he found them—three: one down-canyon, one up-canyon, the third man posted on Ben's side of the flat between Ben and the gallows tree. When the Texan saw him, his pale eyes narrowed.

It was the duty of this guard to watch for any traveler who might be using the side trail on which Ben Allison had come. That the man was watching, instead, the last cruel cinching of the hangman's knot was small dereliction, for the others of the posse were as single-eyed as he. A man might see a score of these rightful executions, yet not ever get broken to the deep-gut feel of them.

Ben had heard the vigilantes talk of this feeling, and it was straight talk; they believed it.

When you hung a man, the vigilantes claimed, you weren't just killing him—you were upholding the law. And the law said the penalty for murder was death at the end of a spinning, jerking rope. Sure, it hit you in the guts every time, but every time you also rode away a better man than you had come and that was where the feeling came in, the feeling of justice done, and a terrible duty stood to without flinching.

That puzzled Ben. To him, the real murderers were the vigilantes themselves—the bastards.

But he was himself too quick with his judgment, too

3

vengeful in his verdict. Dansk Jensen, the guard who sat his mount in the lea of the boulder not ten feet from the crouching Texan, was no killer of innocent boys. He had lost a son to pneumonia this same winter who was no older than the vagrant charged with cleaving the skull of dancehall doxie Billie Dove Vardeen. Jensen understood boys, and loved them. It had hurt him that this lad, no matter what his kind, could kill a white woman with a hand-ax. Neither did it seem that the boy was grown enough to have lustfully committed on Billie Dove the forceful rape Dr. Hankins had said was a part of the crime. Jensen shook his blond head. All prejudice aside, a wandering stray-dog kid like that just didn't up and manhandle a strong healthy young whore, much less leave his name-branded ax-blade buried to the haft between her painted eyes.

Dansk Jensen had wanted a miners' court convened, due to the suspect's age. The court, he said, ought at least to hear the boy's story that he had never been near Billie Dove, far from axing her down or raping her.

The committee's Executive had ruled against him.

The ax did bear his name burned into its handle and the boy did admit to Ruel Oakes being his name. More damning yet, he could find no witness in all of Canyon Creek to support his plea that he had been asleep the entire time of the killing in the shut-down Old Glory mine drift, above town, where he was camping like the outcast mongrel his marked face made him. And Elvira Semple, best friend and working mate of the deceased, positively identified young Oakes as the sneaking "speckled-skinned monster" who had asked her what it would cost just to "talk" to the beautiful Billie Dove. This had been early dusk, approximately an hour before the discovery of the mutilated body.

Although he admitted the conversation with Elvira Semple, the boy insisted again he had never been near her friend.

The stony-faced Executive would not buy the story.

"Get August Wendler and his rope," he ordered.

Jensen, the camp blacksmith and a burly, good-

4

natured Dane, moved uneasily in the saddle as he remembered the pleas of the unknown drifter youth.

Behind the worried blacksmith, Ben Allison glanced at the cloud cover overhead. A quarter-blood Kwahadi Comanche, the tall man could read weather signs as well in far Montana as in the staked plains of home. A blizzard was blowing up which looked like a hard blue norther. Ben had been counting on its arrival to cover his own tracks out of the territory, but now it would have to cover double—double, that was, or nothing. For if he went forward at this point to take the boy from the stranglers, and missed, both of them would hang. "Two more for the sycamore tree," as they said in the camps; he and the boy would dance the airy trot together in old Montana Territory.

Ben's dark lips lifted to a wry grimace.

It was his habit to laugh, rather than grumble, when troublesome currents drove the river into the willows.

Besides, he owed these muddy-booted prospectors something. It might take a bit of paying, at the going rate of two dozen of them to one of him, but Ben had never stood short on an honest debt. His grin was still there when he slid on around the boulder and came up behind the blacksmith.

2

Dansk Jensen knew, in the heartbeat of time when his horse squatted, that someone had vaulted on-to the animal's rump behind him. He even had time to feel the muscular forearm slide like a voice-choking bar across his throat. He remembered opening his mouth to cry out the alarm, and no sound coming forth. Then the darkness descended with the thud of Ben's pistol barrel.

The Texan held Jensen's body in the saddle, reaching around the blacksmith to take the reins as they fell away from the slack hands. Guiding the bay horse with his knees, Indian-style, he calmed him with *hoh-shuh* grunts, getting him safely behind the boulder. Here, he eased Jensen's body to the ground, bridle-tying the bay to a piñon snag some Indian god had planted in just the right rocky hole for his part-Comanche grandson. It required the work of only a minute or two for Ben to strip off the blacksmith's wolf-fur winter coat and ear-flapped felt miner's hat and don them himself. He was only a reasonably good imitation of Dansk Jensen when, in the next moment, he swung up onto the restive animal. But Ben knew well the odds he was betting on.

"All right, horse," he murmured under his breath to the bay, "just walk up slow and edge in among them like we belonged, and our dues was paid. I will think of something better along the way."

He was talking not to the horse, but to himself.

It was a habit of his, a thing that loners picked up—a way of the owlhoot trail. When a man rode that dangerous country alone, he had to think out loud, to "augur it with his pony," as the saying went. It was the high-line rider's way to keep his thinking straight. If he held it inside himself, he wound up truly strange.

"Hoh-shuh," he whispered to the borrowed mount of Dansk Jensen, now clear of the boulder, and heading in apace toward the gnarled sycamore. "Slow up, slow up. I told you to tread gentle." The walking horse flicked back friendly ears, listening, and Ben added with Comanche urgency, *"Ehaitsma, hoh-shuh—!"*

The settlement-reared bay responded to the Indian words, slowing immediately. It was a passing odd fact, Ben knew, that there was magic in the red tongue as far as horses were concerned. Foaled tame or wild, most frontier horses would willingly accept any Indian's approach, while the same animals would kick or bite or buck off an unknown white man. Even quarter-bred

6

redmen, like Ben, possessed a degree of this horse medicine. So it was that the bay came like a shadow to ease unnoted in among the outer ranks of the Canyon Creek possemen and its tall rider was given the last chancy moment in which to reassess the particulars of his arrival among the Vigilantes of Montana. The prospects were not encouraging.

The hanging tree stood over against the far canyon wall. The nightriders formed a half-moon ring about it, two and three horsemen deep, tight in on the doomed prisoner. A small dog could not have broken that circle of hard-eyed humanity without being trampled on, but there *was* one narrow pathway cleared through the packed ranks of the mounted men where the riderless but saddled horse of the Executive stood ready to haul up the youth when signaled. From the horn of this animal's saddle the rope ran over the limb and down to the boy's neck. As Ben watched, sickened, the quirtman, who would on command whip the hanging horse to launch the victim into eternity, was ordered by the Executive to take up the slack. Eagerly, the quirtman did so.

Ben fixed his pale eyes on the posse leader——he would remember *this* Executive. This was the most brutal way possible to hang a man and it gave no chance, such as the "drop" did, for the breaking of the neck in quick mercy. Here the victim would choke to death the long, agonizing, spinning way. He might take several minutes to die. Ben had seen men hung in this inhuman manner jerking for a quarter hour after they were hauled up.

Yes, he would remember *this* Executive.

Ben was puzzled that he didn't know him. He was well acquainted with Nathan Stark, long-time head of the Vigilantes of Montana. Where was Stark now? Who was this bony-jawed substitute? Why hadn't Ben Allison seen him before? Had Nathan Stark quit the committee? Was this rattler-faced Executive a new man who was replacing Stark? Had he been the possible difference in Ben being issued only a one-day pass? Had his first hunch to go see Stark been the true one? Might he thus have won vigilante as well as court clearance?

Too late—much too late to learn that.

The pasteboards were already face-down here. It was cards to the gamblers, and the last stack to shove in.

At the gallows tree, the rope bit squeakingly into the bark of the hanging limb as the long-haired boy uttered a strangulated cry. Only the frayed toes of his work brogans still touched the graveled sand of the creek flat. "She's set," called August Wendler.

"Swing him," ordered the Executive.

"He's swung!" answered the waiting quirtman, and drew back to whip the hanging horse. His arm was still upraised when the bay horse of blacksmith Jensen burst through the vigilante circle into the cleared path of the hanging horse. In the next instant, Ben swung one long leg free of his stirrup and the high cowboy heel of the boot nearly tore off the quirtman's head. The fellow collapsed screaming and Ben, an eight-inch Comanche skinning knife between his bared teeth, slashed the blade across the strumming tightness of the rope while riding at a dead, unbroken gallop.

The familiar bay horse, wolfskin coat, and ear-flapped hat of Dansk Jensen gave the Texan the ten seconds that meant a fighting chance for him and the boy.

"For God's sake, Jensen! You crazy?" he heard a man yell. Then, another shouting, "It's the goddamned blacksmith! Get him down! Knock him off that horse!"

By this time Ben had the bay stopped over the crumpled body of the youth, where it had fallen, rope still around his neck. Spearing downward with one arm, Ben caught the free end of the rope, and literally pulled the choking prisoner up onto the horse by the hangman's noose. Slashing free the boy's hands with the knife, he wheeled their mount toward the vigilante leader's riderless horse.

In the wild milling about and confusion on the gallows tree flat, the Executive of the Canyon Creek

8

Committee also rushed toward the abandoned mount. He came first to the animal and swung aboard him, as Ben spurred up and drove into the horse at full gallop. The two opposing riders froze for a muscle twitch of time.

Ben saw the twisting, blue-stitched scar running from the Executive's heavy brow-ridge down across the left eye to the gaunt cheekbone, where its cruel passage distorted the eye itself into a demonic, never-blinking glare. The other man saw a pair of slanted, fire-gray eyes such as never blazed beneath the blond brow of blacksmith Jensen, and an angular intense face as dark-skinned as that of any horseback Indian.

The Executive's skull-like stare turned ashen.

The drained look was one Ben had never seen before on the face of any man—human hatred so pure, so total, as to border madness. The raging voice matched it.

"Kill him! Kill him! It's not Jensen, you fools!"

"You got that much right, anyway," Ben said quietly as he drew his long-barreled cavalry Colt out of its worn San Saba holster in a snake flick of motion too blurred to trace or evade. The revolver's barrel cracked into the head of the Executive three times and the Montanan toppled from the saddle. Ben had never felt that way about hitting a man: he wanted to kill the vigilante chief, actually to crush his very brains through the bones of his disfigured face. It was all he could do not to follow the Montanan to the ground and finish the job in raging anger.

But the plight of the boy held him, for if Ben went after the downed vigilante leader, there would be no chance for the kid. "Hang onto the horn!" he yelled as he manhandled the youth over into the empty saddle of the Executive. The lad, his mind clearing, clung to leather desperately. Ben, with a Comanche whoop, seized the loose reins of the animal and led it off behind the lumbering bay at a gravel-spraying gallop.

Reaching the shelter of the big boulder, he drove the two horses past it and on up the steep incline of the

9

side canyon. A thin volley of rifle and pistol shots
rattled the rocks about them. Ben replied with his Colt,
firing high and wide. His ricochets seemed to whine off
in a dozen directions, delaying the posse. The pause
gave Ben time to collect his Comanche gelding which
he had left in the mouth of the draw. From there, he
fled with the boy and the augmented three-horse cavalcade away up the blackness of the trail by which he
had come to this place.

There was no immediate pursuit, a fact which reassured the tall man very little. The Canyon Creekers
were professional manhunters and they would not be
long in coming.

Meanwhile, he and the reprieved prisoner likely had
the remainder of the freezing winter night in which to
celebrate their escape.

After that, it was magpies and eyeballs-for-break-
fast time again.

3

The snow began before Ben and the boy were
twenty minutes from the gallows tree flat. It came
down in a suddenly windless, unreal silence, the flakes
as big as wood-ash curls. Ben halted the horses and
peered at the boy, whose face was hidden by Dansk
Jensen's big ear-flapped cap. "You all right?" Ben
asked.

The youth did not reply, but Ben heard the chatter
of his clenched teeth. He went to the Comanche gelding and unstrapped his bedroll to get the blanket. He
wound it around the boy, fastening it with three turns
of his lasso, and then ran the rope in a dally about the
saddlehorn. From there, he took it up through the

snaffle ring of the gray's bridle and then to his own mount's saddle, where he fastened it to a cantle ring.

"You might dangle," he told the boy, "but you ain't going to fall off. Just hang on and let my bay horse tow you. We'll make it, kid."

Still the boy did not reply. They set out with the Comanche pony Puhakat, or Medicine Man, called "Poo Cat" by Ben, moving free in the rear. The mustang would not leave his tall master, for the Indian top horses were like that. They lived with their riders, as did the Arabian horses of the Bedouins, and the loyalties, both ways, were as fierce as the blood of the sharers.

"Wagh!" Ben called to the south-plains gelding. "We're going home."

The gelding snorted and made a throaty chuckling answer that was known only to mustangs and to mustang men.

"Sure enough," said Ben, "we're gone."

He kicked the bay horse into a longer stride. He did not care for the weather; it was the same from the Texas brasada to the buffalo pastures of Montana's Milk River. When the wind fell off like that, it was gathering itself to kill you.

They went on.

Within the first mile, the wind began crying like a lost coyote and in minutes the storm was upon them. An endless two hours later, it had built up to three feet of snow in the drifts and they were trapped.

The bay halted and stood heaving. He was a great and powerful horse, but he was done. Ben felt the chill of more than the Montana snows. Behind him, the boy sensed his hesitation to be more than another rest for the horses. He forced his own mount forward. Again, he did not speak, but Ben understood the wordless language of fear in the boy's instinctive action. "Whoa up. Easy now," he said. "Don't jump that horse like that. Let him be. We'll go along in a minute now. Don't be afeered."

But he was lying to the lad and to himself.

Ben Allison did not know, any more than did the

11

nameless youth beside him, if this was where the vigilantes would find their bones next spring.

Yet he would not break—would not ever admit that they were where he was so vastly afraid they were.

To keep his own nerves from stampeding and frightening the desperate youth he had rescued, he commenced to talk to his silent companion. He began to explain various ways in which blizzards could be beaten and prayed, meanwhile, that any one of those ways would present itself to him, Ben Allison, as a *real* solution.

Hearing his master's wind-buffeted words, the wiry mustang, Poo Cat, came lunging and buck-jumping up through the drifts to Ben's side. Here, he at once began bumping the tall rider with his head, at the same time whinnying demandingly, then backing away a jump or two.

Indian-wise, Ben understood he was being talked to.

"All right," he said, "go ahead. We'll follow you."

But the mustang, wheeling away, did not go ahead.

Rather, he turned back down-canyon toward the way they had just come. Ben shouted after him, but the horse continued. Every few jumps he stopped and whistled imperatively at Ben, as though he were saying, "Come on, come on—!"

Ben was afraid to follow him. They couldn't go back that way because the vigilantes were down there somewhere—storm or no storm. He held the bay in.

The mustang lunged on through the down-canyon snow. He was not stopping any more now, nor whistling back to Ben, who knew it was then or never for going after the Indian pony. Instantly, he made his decision. Kicking the bay around in the trail, he sent him past the gray, at the same time shouting at the boy to hold tight, that Poo Cat had smelled a hole in the wall. With that, the two horses were plowing after the vanishing mustang and within minutes had followed the little Texas pony into what looked like a blank wall of canyon rock.

It proved to be, however, what the Comanches

12

called a "bitch-wolf hole," that is, a blind entrance. The mustang guided the other mounts in behind the false rampart as though foaled in its shelter, threading among huge fallen boulders along an upward-twisting goat track that would have defeated any but mountain-wise horses.

As they climbed, Ben could see nothing above save naked and unbroken cliff. But swiftly, when they topped the granite incline, the Texan's pale eyes widened in disbelief. Before them lay a level meadow of winter-cured grass, with a quantity of dead-and-down firewood as well as live timber, an unfrozen spring for water, and the entire hidden bench sheltered in such a way by the high canyon overhang as to be windless and virtually snow-free. It was the ultimate miracle of what Ben Allison would ever after call Poo Cat's place.

Unroping the boy's gray horse, he turned it loose. The mustang which had led them there nosed the gray as if to be sure it was all right, then tossed his head at Ben and chuckled in his throat.

"Sure enough," said the big man, "I owe you one."

Poo Cat snorted acknowledgment of the debt, and trotted away over the grassy bench toward wood and water. Ben followed on the bay horse of blacksmith Jensen. Left behind, the gray whinnied anxiously and broke into a jarring lope to catch up. On its back, the outcast of Canyon Creek almost, but not quite, lost saddle.

He hung on.

It was all that was left for him to do in Poo Cat's place, or any other place.

4

Ben camped in the timber at the foot of the overhang, hard against the wall of the cliff. It was an owlhoot habit; he knew the Canyon Creek possemen would not be bucking the canyon drifts before daylight, if then. Yet many a good man had died betting on what he knew. Old wolves, like Ben Allison, always lay up where nothing could come around behind them. That was how they got to be old wolves.

While Ben began gathering wood, the boy got off the gray and crawled in under the overhang. Ben found him there a few minutes later, shuddering with cold and weariness. "Be easy," he told him. "There ain't nothing going to harm you no more."

But still the youth did not speak. Frowning, Ben made a smokeless Indian fire, then lit it with a match and a handful of rock moss. It burned with a clear flame and would last the night through with no more than a stick or three to hold it, once it was banked. It would be there in the morning, too, needing only more moss and the fan of a man's hat under a pitchpine chunk to break it into usable flame once more. "Injun fire," Ben explained to the boy. "You mark how it's done and you ain't never going to freeze for want of wood or starter."

The other said nothing, and only drew the blanket higher around his shadowed face.

Ben unsaddled and turned loose the horses, got his bedroll and took from it a coffeepot and a battered cup. When the fire settled in, he would brew a pot for the boy and himself. That would thaw out the kid's tongue. Coffee was next to blood in need. The grind Ben used, half mocha, half java, was called jamoka back home in Texas. It made a brew thick enough to float a bullet, black enough to write a letter home, and was to a wet or bone-chilled drover what Taos rotgut was to a drunken Comanche Indian. The mere imagining of its delights cheered up the tall cowboy as he relaxed against the warming rock of the overhang and, finally, fell asleep.

When he awakened, the boy had ground the beans and brewed the coffee for him, and it was broad-breaking daylight there in Poo Cat's place.

"Morning!" Ben called cheerily. He stretched the rock-induced ache out of his bones. "Going to be a beautiful day, yonder."

The youth glanced at him warily from under the cover of blacksmith Jensen's cap which he wore low against the first frostiness of daybreak. He neither replied to Ben's greeting nor affirmed the weather forecast. Ben said nothing. He joined the boy at the fire and held out the cup for filling. The youth hesitated, keeping his face turned away, but then he took up the pot and poured. He had to look at Ben when he did this and the tall man saw his companion's face for the first time in good light.

It was then he knew what the vigilantes knew.

The boy was a mulatto, a light-colored, freckled Negro. What the whites of the frontier called, unfeelingly, a speckled nigger. But that was not all of it: he was *now* Ben Allison's speckled nigger.

The implications of the realization would have shaken any white man in that time and place, and Ben was hit low and hard. He did not break, however.

"Yes sir," he repeated, swishing his cup and looking around at the grand solitude of the canyon. "It's going to be a beautiful day."

From under the bill of the miner's cap, the mulatto youth studied his benefactor. He saw that Ben was a lean, muscular man whose every line and movement spelled a born horseman. The big Texan showed hair as long and unshorn as that of his observer. But Ben's was the color of a mountain-lion pelt, all pale yellows

15

with tawny streakings, yet still thick and hanging straight the way an Indian's hair did. He wore his black Stetson as an Indian would, jammed flat on his head, and he was dressed like an Indian with elkhide leggins and buffalo coat. Finally, though, it was the Indian-dark face itself which pinned the memory. It was a menacing face, yet steady with sane judgment, and the mulatto boy suddenly felt a great weight of fear lift from him.

Seeing this look of glad relief in his companion's features, Ben poured himself another cup of coffee and used the drinking of it to cover his own study of the boy he had saved from the Vigilantes of Montana. In seeming mid-examination, he said unexpectedly, "All right, kid. You want to tell me about it?"

Instantly, the fear was back on the boy's face. Leaping up, he ran out onto the open bench. The horses, startled by his dash, spooked and raced away. He stood a moment—bewildered, twisting this way and that, looking for a place to run to. Then, remembering that for him there was no such other place, he turned and came haltingly back to the fire. Head lowered, he stood a moment, then looked Ben directly in the eye.

"I didn't do it," he said.

"*Hoh-shuh,* kid," Ben said. "I ain't your judge." Then, softly, "What is it you ain't done?"

The boy stared at Ben in surprise. He had trusted the big white man. Now Ben was tricking him—acting gentle while demanding the answer to the same hanging question as the possemen.

"What did you do and how came you to do it?"

It wasn't any different than it had been in Canyon Creek under the glare of Selman Draco. And the friendless boy had no better answer for it here than there. As a result, the hurt and confused youth gave Ben no answer at all.

"Well," insisted the latter, "what was it?"

The freckled face grew desperate again, its set of pain and fatigue deepening, and briefly returned hope, violated so quickly, vanished altogether. The mulatto lad sank wordlessly to the rock by the fire. He

16

did not weep tears, but rather shed them in dry, wracking shudders. Ben understood then that it was the only answer the boy would furnish for the time, and he did not like it.

He was determined to be fair, yet he could not find anything more of helpful counsel to give the youngster than he already had. Sure, the poor devil said he didn't do it, whatever *it* was. But he had not convinced Ben, and the tall cowboy would not lie to him about it.

The seeds of real suspicion had been sown; they would have to grow up green or drought out brown along the way of the run for the Wyoming line.

5

They had an hour before it happened.

Innocently, they used the time for a dawdling breakfast of thick bacon slices, pan-fried biscuit bread, and a second pot of fragrant Texas jamoka. Ben believed that the way to loosen any human tongue was to feed the stomach well. He had seen it work with many a hardcase in his time—and many a frightened weaker man, as well. He also understood that a starter was often needed, and to get the boy to open up he laid an encircling trail of talk.

"Well," he said, pouring the last of the coffee for his companion, "it's baptizing time."

"Huh?" blinked the boy.

"Time for the two of us to give ourselves names," Ben grinned. "You can use the one you already got, or pick a ringer to suit your fancy. Mine's Ben Allison."

"Your real one?"

"Yep."

The boy eyed him. "Mine's Ruel Oakes," he said.

17

Ben nodded. "I don't need to ask you if it's your Bible brand. A man can tell when a friend is leveling."

The dirty-faced youth shook his head. "I ain't no friends," he said.

"All right. That ain't the same as saying I ain't got any."

"It don't make sense, you calling me your friend."

"What you want me to call you?"

"Ruel, I reckon."

"It's a good name. How you going to call me?"

The boy really didn't know. He frowned over it and said, "Mister will do, won't it, mister?"

"No," said the tall man. "I ain't been mister to anybody that was my friend. You want me to call you Ruel, then I allow you're just going to have to call me Ben. It's a heap easier to spell than mister."

He looked at the boy, head cocked.

"You know how to spell mister, Ruel?"

The ragged drifter returned his look, and shook his head again. "Don't know how to spell Ben, neither," he mumbled.

"Leastways," Ben said, "you know how to say it."

They sat some more.

The boy was not going to talk; Ben laid another line of tracks for him, his smiles all gone now.

He began by telling the youth that they, the two of them, were in the same predicament. Both had a murder charge against them, put there by the same bunch of night-riding vigilantes. In this way, there was no need for Ruel Oakes to feel he owed Ben Allison any more than what Ben Allison would have done for any man he found being judged by the Montana stranglers. It wasn't, Ben said, like Ruel Oakes was anything special. The only difference between him and Ben Allison was that Ben Allison had been tried by a real judge and found innocent of any crime. Ruel had been indicted by the vigilantes, who never gave anyone a real trial. But Ben still didn't know, no man knew, whether or not Ruel Oakes was likewise innocent of his crime.

"I done told you," the boy interrupted.

"Sure," said Ben, "I heard you."

A pause ensued, the boy's face growing furtive and uneasy again. This big, mean-looking rider was not going to believe him, no matter what he said. It was the same thing all over again as with the posse from Canyon Creek. You told them you didn't do it and they just looked at you and nodded and said, "Sure, you didn't."

But Ben wasn't giving up yet.

The thing was, he told the boy, that they were together in this trouble—like it or not, believe each other or suspect each other or whatever. The vigilantes weren't after only Ruel Oakes or only Ben Allison. They were after *them*. "If they catch up to us, now, boy," Ben finished, "they're going to kill us. That's all you got to put into your hard nigger head, you hear? You don't hanker to die, you do what I tell you. Understand?"

The youth shook his head. "I dunno," he said.

Ben nodded. "I'll tell you one thing you don't know," he scowled. "That's them vigilantes. Boy, wasn't that you they was hanging back yonder to the gallows tree? Was that somebody else I seen all fish-gut gray in the face? And with that noose-knot bringing the blood back of his off ear? I'd of swore it was you that I cut down and drug out'n there by the rope halter they had putten on you. Reckon maybe the bad light fooled me."

The pale gray eyes probed the mulatto boy's face.

"Ruel Oakes," the tall rider said, low-voiced, "either you done what the stranglers said you done, or you are the stupidest one colored kid ever to come West out'n the settlements."

Again the pause, the pale eyes probing.

"Now you better give me your pick of them two ways to go, right sudden. You don't, and I'm going to hoist you back on the Executive's horse to go your own trail."

For a moment, it seemed the youth would bound up

and run off again. But something in the dark face studying him across the drift smoke of the breakfast embers reminded him of his earlier confidence in the sinister-looking Texas man, and suddenly he broke.

The story of Billie Dove Vardeen's brutal killing rushed out of him, together with his own thin defense of the finding of his name-branded hand-ax buried in the prostitute's forehead. The story did not sound notably better to Ben than it had to the grim-jawed vigilantes. It was not, certainly, the kind of evidence you hung a man on without sifting it considerably and damned carefully. But it was damning. If you just looked at it and looked at the dead whore, and this dirty, hangdog, drifter kid, and if the kid acted the selfsame butt-headed, shifty-eyed way that he had been acting with you, why then you commenced to understand how the posse came to be in the canyon. Sitting on any due and legal jury in the frontier world, Ben Allison would never have voted to hang the boy and never voted to turn him loose, either. Just listening to the kid, now—just watching him twist and gulp and look away, and stammer for his words—Ben knew suddenly, and with enormous surprise, how it was that the vigilantes felt the way they did.

It wasn't whether or not the trial they gave their captives was conducted in a fair and thorough way; it was only if the accused had done what they had caught him for doing.

Had the kid killed the whore or hadn't he?

That was the total question, its answer all too evident. Yet, while reaching the guilty verdict in his mind, Ben could not agree to it in his heart. Damn it, it still mattered that the prisoner have his say listened to by a jury of decent people in open daylight court. More than that, time ought to be granted to gather evidence both ways, and to let tempers cool down and the folks on the jury be sure they had the right suspect for the crime charged.

For Ben, another answer loomed.

That wasn't just some whipped and kicked-around

20

colored boy, unlucky enough to be half-white, that the stranglers had been going to hang back yonder in the main canyon last midnight.

It was Ben Allison, too.

6

Ben waited for the mulatto boy to make his choice of trails. He knew it was hard doing, and knew also that there was no other way. The boy knew this as well.

"I'm a'going with you," he said, "long as I kin."

The big rider nodded.

"Kid," he warned, "we got even a worse way to ride than I figured. There ain't no other trail for us. It don't matter if we had thirty horses and Wyoming wasn't but three jumps down the line. They ain't going to leave us make it—not me and you, they ain't."

The boy leaned forward intently. "How so is that? Ain't we already as good as got away?" he asked.

"Not hardly, we ain't," Ben answered sternly. "Somebody else they might let up on, once shut of Montana. But me having put them to shame, and you being black and that whore white, they will plaster paper on us against every hoosegow wall between here and San Antone. It's no difference what we do, once them flyers is pasted up. Even a dumb Injun can read M-U-R-D-E-R and R-A-P-E and N-I-G-G-E-R. If it happens the stranglers offers halfways decent reward money on us, me and you ain't no chance of making it to Texas. You understand?"

"Surely I do," said the mulatto softly. "It ain't me and you don't have no chance; it's only me."

21

"No sir!" Ben denied instantly. "Now you listen to me, Ruel Oakes. You quit thinking like that!"

The big cowboy was aroused. The boy caught the scent of his anger and swung his head up once more.

"We got to fight the bastards, kid," Ben said, gritting his teeth. "You hear? We keep running, we're done for. If the vigilantes don't get us, the bounty hunters will. If they miss, the magpies are waiting. We're going back to Canyon Creek and get you a fair trial. That's your chance, boy. Your only one."

"Back to Canyon Creek? They'll string us sure!"

"That's *my* chance," Ben said quietly. "I'm taking it to find out who really kilt your whore, and maybe my storekeeper, but it's cat and mousy, I'll grant you."

"Cat and mousy, Mr. Ben?"

"Look at it this way," nodded Ben. "Say the stranglers is the cat. Who you reckon is the mice?"

"Why, we is!" replied the youth proudly. Then, realizing what he had suggested: "We *is?*" he gulped.

The inflection of the query, the sudden deflation of the youngster's returning hopes, the honesty with which he had blurted out the problem—hit Ben just so. The wide Indian mouth lifted over white teeth.

"Damned if we ain't, Ruel Oakes," he laughed.

Then, rewarded by seeing the new belief in their partnership show again in the boy's face, Ben got up from the fire feeling his own confidence bolstered.

"Come along on," he said to the youth. "Let's gird up and get shut of this canyon, before they bottle both ends of it on us."

"Can we get through the snow?"

"We'll do it easy with the horses fresh. We ain't but three miles to go. And unless the posse spent the night breaking trail for one another, they got the full way to come from the main canyon. With tired horses."

"How we know they ain't tried it?"

"We don't," Ben grinned. "We'll just have to chance it. Come on, catch up the gray for yourself. I'll get the other two."

Partly reassured, the boy helped with the horses and the work of putting out and scattering the fire, all com-

22

pleted with Indian thoroughness by the tall man. "Got to leave our mother's bones the way we find them," he told the boy.

"Your mother's bones?" The boy eyed him dubiously.

"Injun talk," Ben explained. "The mother is the earth. Her bones is anything in that earth, or that grows atop it. You put it all back the way it was when you made your camp. That way, you ain't done no harm for the next one comes this way. Understand?"

The boy shook his head, and then swung up awkwardly on the tall gray horse. "We didn't do no harm here," he said.

"You ain't an Injun," Ben answered.

He got up on Poo Cat; the bay was on the lead as packhorse and spare. "All right," he said, waving. "Let's get at them drifts, yonder." He started the Texas pony for the bench trail down to the outer canyon. As they went, the birds, which had been silent for an unnoticed several minutes, began anew their noisy chatter at the departing aliens. "Them damned jays," laughed Ben to the boy. "Always got something to say about nothing."

The youth glanced up at the birds in question, now circling out over the bench trail and above the canyon.

"Dunno, Mr. Ben," he corrected frowningly, "but them don't looken like jaybirds to me; them's magpies."

Ben stiffened as though a cherry-red running iron had been put into him, straight up. But it was too late and the drifter kid was right. They *were* magpies.

They stopped at the head of the bench trail, the three horses bunched in an unordered halt, crowding one another. In the utter stillness, the rocks that were kicked into motion by the nervously-moving feet of the horses sounded to Ben and his companion like an avalanche cascading down toward the outer canyon. Some of the dislodged stones were still trickling downward when the familiar flat voice of the vigilante leader rasped upward.

23

"You up there, stranger—you and the nigger boy come out peaceful or we come in unpeaceful. It's your free choice. You got ten minutes."

The gray horse, recognizing the voice of its owner, whinnied loudly into the following silence.

"Ten minutes," the Executive repeated tonelessly.

After that only the wind was heard muttering in the outer canyon and up on the bench. Ben and the mulatto youth stared at one another, each knowing what was passing through the other's mind. They were as trapped together as the boy had been alone. Poo Cat's place was the same as the gallows tree flat.

Two more for the sycamore, sure enough.

All thanks to big Ben Allison.

7

Ben had been an outlaw for too many winters in those hard times caused by the War Between the States to sit very long listening to the wind.

Finger to his lips, he motioned the mulatto boy to slide off his horse. He set the example by dismounting and leading the Comanche pony back into the boulders away from the drop-off. The boy followed with the gray and Ben, giving him a quick pat of approval on his back, said to him, "Ruel Oakes, you're the new horse holder for this gang." Giving over the reins of his gelding and the lead rope of the bay packhorse, he added sharply, "I don't want you should budge from here, understand?"

The youth nodded and took a tight grip on all three horses. He was frightened and wanted to say something, but Ben was already gone, running to the drop-off. Once there, he bellied down among the small float rock and cupped his hands to call below.

"Hello, down there! Who am I talking to?"

"Canyon Creek Vigilance Committee," answered a voice that was not the Executive's. "Who's asking?"

"Ben Allison, San Saba, Texas."

"Allison, you say? Ain't you the one turned loose in Bozeman yesterday? Feller that murdered John Fisher on the Boise Road? For ten thousand paper cash?"

"Yes and no."

"Which you saying?"

"Yes, I'm the one turned loose in Bozeman. No, I ain't the feller murdered nobody on no road for no money."

The windy stillness returned.

"Allison." It was the other voice again, not the Executive's. "What's your deal?"

"A miners' court," said Ben. "Open and in daylight—to hear both me and the colored kid."

"We can't give you any guarantees."

"Yes, you can. Fetch Nathan Stark and lawyer Lazarus out here. Me and the boy will surrender to them."

Again the windy gusts of unbroken silence. And Ben knew why.

There was no reason for the committeemen to go get Stark; hanging authority rode with every such party that set out from the camps. As the vigilantes saw these matters, the mulatto drifter and his Texas rescuer were guilty; they had brought their rope and they intended to use it on Ruel Oakes *and* Ben Allison.

Ben, not liking the silence, cupped his hands once more.

"You going to fetch Stark, or ain't you?"

"Not likely—Stark's in Kansas City buying herd bulls and Lazarus won't act with him away. Forget it."

"Allison." It was the Executive's flat voice, back again. "I gave you ten minutes. You've wasted six. You can subtract, can't you?"

25

"Sure," said the tall cowboy. "Six from ten leaves two. Me and the kid."

"Not necessarily," answered the flat voice. "Try one from two."

"Which one?" said Ben, scowling.

He could hear the buzz of discussion below which followed, then it was the unknown posseman's voice coming up the switchback trail to the bench.

"Mr. Draco says you deliver out the nigger and he will send two men to ride you to the Wyoming line, not follering you over it."

"Who's Mr. Draco?"

"The Executive."

"Allison." It was the flat voice. "Three minutes."

"Draco?"

"Yes?"

"How do I know your men won't sack me this side of Wyoming?"

"You don't."

"Then I better."

"How so?"

"You got us boxed up here, Mr. Draco, true? The trail, however, is one horse wide. You ain't coming up here and we ain't coming down there, without good men die for nothing. That is, unless you make a deal."

It was his one hole card and Ben played it with grave doubts. The vigilantes could stand guard in shifts all winter long. Up on the bench, Ben and Ruel had food for maybe a week, and at that they would be starving from the first day. But Ben's hole card did not so much depend on a starve-out. The stranglers would have to win that. The other thing was—how anxious was somebody down there to hang the mulatto drifter? And Ben had guessed right!

"Allison." It was the other voice. "Mr. Draco is sending up a volunteer hostage. You hold your weapon on him, until you're safe in Wyoming. Mr. Draco says there's nine minutes gone on your clock."

A volunteer hostage, Ben thought. One of the posse members? The vigilantes wanted Ruel Oakes that bad?

26

No, Ben didn't believe it. Not for that dancehall trollop, a pathetic painted thing who was for sale every night. Her price was a mine-run nugget or a measly pinch of dust, not a rusted camp-ax in the middle of her head. No sir, something was leaking in the sluicebox here.

"Allison." It was Draco's ominous voice. "Thirty seconds."

"I'm thinking!" cried Ben. "It ain't easy."

"You can make it easy; we want that nigger and we want him now."

"Goddamn them," Ben muttered. He didn't like them always calling the poor kid a nigger, like that. Sure, he was a nigger—Ruel Oakes knew that better than anybody. But they were making it sound as though being a nigger was what the poor damned kid was guilty of, and Ben Allison knew better than that. Nigger was the excuse to make it quick and full of anger; it wasn't the real reason.

But what *was* the real reason the stranglers had outmarched him? Their move up the canyon at the risk of their lives made no manhunting sense. Granted, the Vigilantes of Montana were known for never giving up a trail. Granted, too, that Ben had not expected them to give up on this one. He had even warned the mulatto kid about it an hour ago. But if Ben had that same getaway trail to ride again from gallows tree flat, he would still do it, figuring the possemen never to follow them up the trail on the same night in a heavy snow. Still, the posse had done it and Ben had been wrong and, if he did not play his next pasteboard squarely on the money, he would be dead wrong.

"Hello, the posse!" he called. "Send up my hostage."

There was a sound of horses grunting and men making subdued talk, and then a mounted man rode out from the canyon side of the blind hole into Poo Cat's place. He was a big man on a borrowed horse and he rode the animal up the steep bench trail with a great deal of care.

Ben saw his size and the white gleam of the blood-soaked bandage around his square blond head, and thought instantly, Look out! This isn't right!

For it was Dansk Jensen, the blacksmith of Canyon Creek.

Vengeance, Ben thought. The son of a bitch wants his chance to get his. You like to killed him with that pistol over the back of his hat, and he's offered to ride under your gun because of it.

The lanky Texan scowled.

All right, then, let him try it. Next time it wouldn't be the back of his hat bent in; it would be the back of his head blown off. As Ruel Oakes did not know the Vigilantes of Montana, so the Vigilantes of Montana did not know Ben Allison. It was a fair hand.

"Blacksmith," he called down to the laboring Canyon Creek rider. "Don't try nothing. It ain't your game."

Jensen merely looked up at the rocks above, among which Ben was hidden.

"Ya, sure," he said. "How is the boy?"

Surprised by the question, Ben looked around automatically to check on Ruel Oakes. The bay and the gray and the Comanche pony were right where Ben had ordered them to be, but that was about it.

Ruel Oakes was gone.

8

Ben let out his held breath slowly between clenched teeth.

He had trusted a colored kid he did not even know, a nameless drifter charged with rape and murder by at least two dozen established citizens of a nearby mining community. And here was his pay. Son of a bitch.

Angrily, he waited for the plodding Jensen to top the bench trail. When the latter did so, he ordered him off his horse, hands spread flat against a big rock. But the Canyon Creeker had no hideout weapon, only a stockman's pocketknife, which Ben permitted him to keep.

"I still figure you for a ringer," Ben growled at him. "If you think your head hurts from the pistol-whipping back yonder, just try your luck again. Understand?"

The blacksmith touched his head bandage and winced, nodding.

Ben jabbed him with the Winchester.

"Walk ahead of me," he snapped. "I've got your horse."

Reaching the other horses in the farther rocks, Jensen, looking around with a frown, said, "Where is the colored boy?"

"Good question," admitted Ben. "The only trouble is I ain't no good answer for it. I left him here holding the horses."

The burly blacksmith shook his head. "Nah, you too smart. You put him in the rocks with a gun."

The mention of the weapon jarred Ben and he looked quickly at the saddle of the bay horse. The Executive's nice new Winchester rifle was not in its scabbard.

"Yep," he nodded, "sure enough I did."

"Ya, well?"

"Ya, well," Ben imitated, "I didn't do it a'purpose. He's swiped the damned thing and run off, whiles I was yonder palavering with you bastards."

Dansk Jensen nodded slowly. He had a broad tanned face, pale blue eyes, golden blond hair shot with iron-gray, was homely as sin and, in his dumb plodding way, nearly as attractive. Ben could not dislike him. Jensen was like the ugliest pup in a litter—beautiful in his own way, the last one to find a home, and the best dog among his brothers and sisters.

"Ya," he now said to Ben, "you was surprised?"

"Lots of times, blacksmith."

"I mean the boy. Sure he run off. He was hearing you sell him to the Committee, ya?"

29

It hit Ben like a forty-four special that was sawed off flat across the nose. Of course! The dumb skowegian was right. The boy *had* heard him dickering with the Executive and the posse. It must have sounded to him as though his self-elected benefactor was selling him out like Judas at that last big barbecue.

"Smithy," he said earnestly to Dansk Jensen, "I reckon you're right, but you ain't right, understand?"

Jensen blinked. "Say what you was meaning."

"The kid," said Ben. "I wasn't going to traitor on him. Not never. It just sounded thataway."

"Ya, sure," agreed the blacksmith, "it did."

Ben looked off over the bench, scanning the timber, cliffbase boulders, and the rise of sheer walls themselves. Nowhere was there any movement or sound to give away the presence of a human being. "Nobody can beat a colored boy on hiding," the tall man said to Dansk Jensen, "but we got to find the poor bastard. He ain't no chanct by hisself."

Jensen's wide blue eyes clouded with slow doubt.

"He is like me," he told Ben. "He don't understand it."

"Don't understand what?" demanded Ben irritably.

"What you say about not betraying him."

"Ahhh," said Ben slowly, feeling the bite of the simple man's truth. "Smithy, in better days for the two of us, you'd have done to breast the high water with."

"Ya? Where was the water?"

Ben scowled hard at him. "All right, let it drift," he said. "Just remember why Draco sent you up here and why he agreed to keep the posse down below: You're their earnest money. Paid for delivery of Ruel Oakes."

"You really give the boy up to them, ya?"

Ben did not answer. His narrowed eyes were studying what appeared to be a spiderweb trail up the face of the wall behind the bench timber. "Up there," he said, pointing. Dansk Jensen sighed heavily, and said, "Ya, I think so," and the two men set out quickly.

In the mind of Dansk Jensen were thoughts unknown. In Ben Allison's mind dwelled a solitary fear; if he did not get Ruel Oakes, the vigilantes would, and Ben was not going to let them take the mulatto boy from him. He had promised him his freedom or a fair trial for same—no more, and no less, than would be coming to any man accused of murder. That was Ben's guarantee.

It contained a single, important clause.

The Vigilantes of Montana were going to find out that Ben K. Allison, of San Saba, Texas, did not make deals he could not keep.

Black or white.

9

Ben and the blacksmith came out of the bench timber, and began the climb over slide rock to the foot of the spiderweb trail. Arriving there, Ben knelt down and read the sign his Comanche years made clear to him. Too clear.

"The boy came this way," he told his companion, "and so did something else. There's bear sign overlaid with boy sign here. Damn."

"Bear?"

"Old Ephraim hisself," Ben said. "Grizzly bear."

Dansk Jensen returned his look. "I will go up for the boy anyway," he said.

Ben shook his head. "Slack off, Smithy," he ordered. "I dunno. Tracks are old, but they run only one way. Up. Could mean there's trail clean to the rim. Could mean dead-end track with a hibernating hole for shut-off."

"Where the bear sleeps for the winter, ya?"

"Well, sort of," amended Ben. "You see, old Eph, he

31

don't go the entire hog of it on that long winter's nap stuff. He sort of hibernates and he sort of don't hibernate. Ain't like other bears. Understand?"

"You mean now he can be asleep, now waking up?"

"Percisely," agreed Ben. "It ain't healthy for nosy human folk to ask him which, neither."

Jensen's blue eyes clouded. "The boy might wake him up," he announced. "We got to hurry."

Ben levered the .44 Winchester, warning the worried blacksmith with a wave of its octagon barrel.

"Hold it," he said. *"We?"*

The Canyon Creeker blinked and nodded. "Ya, we," he answered quietly. "You. Me. We are all the boy has, mister." He moved closer to Ben, and put his hand on the tall cowboy's shoulder. "You trust Jensen," he said. "You let him go up there. You watch here."

Ben was suddenly uneasy. Time had fled swiftly. It was cards to the gamblers again.

"Blacksmith," he decided, "I'd sooner bet a million-dollar poke of pure dust on you than three dried peas on that bad-eyed Executive out yonder in the canyon. Lay your tracks up that trail, but keep a lookout for old Ephraim. And remember the colored kid's got a loaded rifle. Don't push neither of them, hear? I'll caution him you're coming up."

The brawny Dane thanked him, turned at once, and started back up the spiderweb trail. Ben cupped hands, and pitched his voice in guarded tones to the silent cliff above.

"Boy, this-here feller coming up to talk to you is your friend. He's the blacksmith from back yonder to Canyon Creek. The one stood up for you with the vigilantes. Remember? You listen to him, Ruel Oakes."

No answering sound came other than that of Dansk Jensen slipping and sliding upward along the shelflike trail toward its last blind turning above. Ben frowned and cupped his hands again.

"Ruel Oakes, you quit playing nigger on me. Come

the hell down out of them rocks. Answer up now, if you hear me. I got to head back to watch the posse."

There was a final sliding of rock from above, as the blacksmith made the blind turn and disappeared around it, then silence again. Into that silence, however, came a voice in answer to Ben's plea. It did not come from the cliff above, but from the edge of the timber directly behind Ben. It was a flat, nasal voice in a deadly monotone, buzzing like rattler coils.

"No need to worry about the posse, Allison," it said. "Just drop your gun and turn around slow."

The big Texan froze. That was the Executive's voice. The posse, taking advantage of the diversion they knew would be created by their hostage, had followed Jensen. They had sneaked up to the bench from the outer canyon and had Ben cold. He had let them get behind him. Ben Allison was getting old.

But not, he thought desperately, apt to get much older. Still, a man had his pride.

"Nope," he answered the Executive. "I drop my gun, you'll drill me in the back. You other men, don't shoot. I ain't going to."

In the total stillness which ensued, the dark-faced highline rider came slowly about to face his enemies. He did not raise the muzzle of the brass-framed Winchester from its dangling position in his right hand. He spread his booted feet the least bit, pale eyes sweeping the pack of them.

When he spoke, the Texas drawl fell softly.

"All right," he said across the silence which separated him from the Vigilantes of Montana, "it's a new deal, Mr. Draco. Your deck."

Dansk Jensen toiled up the spiderweb trail beyond the blind turn. He could not see Ben Allison below nor could Ben see him now. Ahead, the trail went into a forty-five-degree incline, almost too steep to climb. Jensen clawed his way up it, using both hand and foot. When he reached the top, the trail leveled out and ran some distance back into a tremendous fissure in the rock of the main cliff. It looked to the blacksmith as though only final blackness ended the gloomy pathway far back in the throat of the great cleavage. The hole of the grizzly bear? From his position, Jensen could not answer the fearful question nor, indeed, know if Ruel Oakes were up there.

"Hello!" he called. "You up there, boy?"

Only his own echoes answered him. Again and again he called, but there was no reply. Jensen became frightened. The mulatto lad might not even be up there. Jensen himself had nearly gone over the edge of the cliff trail a half-dozen times. The boy could have fallen and be wedged far down in the pit's darkness in the giant splitting of mother rock below. But the only way to *know* for certain if he had fallen or was up there with the bear—if there were a bear—was to go forward into the yawning chasm.

Dansk Jensen was no hunter, no scout, no student of the mountain frontier. It was simply the measure of the blacksmith as a man that he got up and went on toward the waiting blackness ahead. He had covered most of the distance, enough to see that there was indeed a cave entrance at the ending of the trail, when the voice of the young drifter spoke sharply from unseen cover. "Don't come no farther, Mister Vigilante," the boy warned. "Now please don't you do it."

The Canyon Creek man then did his best with words to persuade the fugitive to give up, to come on back with him and face justice. This time it would be different; Dansk Jensen could guarantee it. Half the men in the original posse that had tried to hang Ruel Oakes had gone home from gallows tree flat convinced that their Executive was a driven man and must be replaced. Only the true fanatics had remained, under the urging of Draco, to trap the boy and the Texas cowman on the bench. Even some of these had told Jensen they were no longer sure of Draco, but were afraid to buck him. The blacksmith promised the mulatto youth that he, Dansk Jensen, now pledged his safety. They would all go back to Canyon Creek and Ruel Oakes would get the fair trial by a miners' court denied him by Draco and the committee.

34

"Boy," called the blacksmith, "it is your very best chance. If you do not take it, they will hunt you down. Come on, now. We must hurry. The cowboy is waiting for us."

But Ruel Oakes would not come down from the cave.

The cowboy, he said, talking to Dansk Jensen, had betrayed him. He could never trust him again. He would rather die where he was. The stranglers would kill the blacksmith, then the cowboy and then him. No. From where he had come to, in the great cave, Ruel Oakes could see the faint light of freedom glowing far behind in the fearful bowel of the cavern. He thanked the blacksmith and knew he was a good man. He remembered him from Canyon Creek. But Ruel Oakes was going on to freedom.

At this point, just as Jensen was about to warn of the possibility of the grizzly at hibernation in the cavern behind the boy—he had located the latter's voice in the big rocks just outside the black hole of the apparent den—the unmistakable deep-gutted rumbling of a disturbed, and very large, meat-eating animal came moaningly from the cave.

In the same instant and responding to the frightening sound, young Oakes burst from the den-mouth boulders to halt uncertainly in the middle of the trail.

"Boy!" shouted Dansk Jensen. "For God's sake—run!"

Another guttural growling issued from the cavern and Ruel Oakes did run. He ran the only way that he might and not find old Ephraim barring his path. The blacksmith caught him in his great arms, as the youth panted up, disarming him before he might think to protest or even try to shoot the Canyon Creek blacksmith.

Both of them, for the moment, looked back up the trail to the den of the grizzly. But the growlings up there had softened off into a muted mumbling and grumbling which, while it seemed to shake the very rocks in which the two crouched, waiting, did not evidently presage issuance of old Eph from his winter sleep.

Jensen lowered the Winchester he had taken from the mulatto youth. "I will keep it," he said, in his simple way. "The bear may yet bound out after us." He looked upward at the black hole of the cave. "We must hurry, my young friend," he added. "Here, give me your hand. Help me down this steep part."

He slung the rifle by its shoulder strap, and offered his hand to Ruel Oakes. The boy, after a puzzled stare at the Canyon Creek blacksmith, took the big hand and, together, they commenced the plunging descent of the spiderweb trail. They went swiftly, too, yet had covered but half the return way when a distant burst of rifle fire cannonaded the rockbound ledge of the trail with ear-splitting reverberations.

"The cowboy!" gasped Dansk Jensen. "Run, boy!"

In a few minutes, they had come to the rear of the blind turn. Here, before rounding the cliff into view of the bench, Jensen halted the mulatto lad.

"Boy," he said pantingly, "the Texas man may be dead now. I want you to know what he told me. He said he never intended to betray you. That was only a deal to save both of your lives. He told me he had a way to do it. He thought you were the one who betrayed him by running away when he had trusted you with the horses. He would want you to know all that."

Ruel Oakes scowled unhappily. "I heard what he said, Mister Blacksmith. Ain't no use to twist it up. Iffen you will give me the gun again, I'll go back up yonder and taken my chances with the b'ar."

Dansk held the rifle away. "No," he said. "I will hold the gun and guard you with it down there myself, all the way back to Canyon Creek. If any man tries to harm you, I will shoot him. Go around the cliff, now, boy. I am behind you."

"You certain sure you won't give me the gun?"

"No, boy. If I must, I will use it to make you go down there. Don't you understand? This thing I have to do this way. It is for me, too, not only you."

Ruel Oakes shook his long, dirty head of hair.

He did not understand anything except that the powerful blacksmith had the Winchester and the Winchester had a shell in the chamber and was cocked. He started around the blind turn. Jensen followed him. Three long steps took them both into open view of the bench below. The blacksmith saw that Ben Allison was still there where he had left him.

But he was not alone any more.

And the hunted eyes of Ruel Oakes opened wide to their bloodshot whites. Beside him, the eyes of Dansk Jensen also opened wide in mute dismay.

It was the end for all of them.

10

Ben Allison waited, his bowed legs braced in the loose rubble of the slide, Winchester hanging in his hand. It was one of those wind-whisper moments in a man's life when he betook his innermost thoughts to trails of yesterday.

When, or where, had Ben gone wrong?

At what turning of the road had he taken the sour fork? He had lucked through four years of the war, and nearing two on the outlaw ridges, plus the five months of a Texas-to-Montana trail drive. He had swum rivers in full flood, hanging onto the tail of a ridden-out horse. He had broken jails and bent laws and busted up jawbones from Red River to the Big Muddy. Was this the mother-end of it?

Across from the cowboy outlaw, Draco and his seven stranglers took their pauses as well. The Texan had called them and they were thinking to raise or to get out. Draco decided to do neither, but to pass.

"Allison," he challenged. "You can't get all of us."

Ben nodded dark-faced agreement.

"I don't want all of you, Mr. Draco. Just you, and maybe your chief assistant."

Draco flicked his good eye to his left, taking in the head-bandaged figure, the man who had seconded him in the canyon parlay, the hanging-horse man. The scarred face writhed into what was supposed to be a smile.

"Mr. Allison, Mr. Fleeger," the bony Executive said, waving. "But I think you two have met before."

A look of hatred, nearly as pure as the one Ben had seen on the leader's distorted features, surged over the face of the hanging-horse man, but he kept silent.

"Can't recall the name," Ben said, "but the face is familiar. My bootheel remembers it from somewheres."

No more smiles now, twisted or straight. The members of the abbreviated posse began to edge away from one another, spreading the target for Ben.

"Wouldn't do that, friends," the cowboy advised.

The possemen stopped and looked at Draco.

Draco exchanged looks with Fleeger.

Fleeger glanced away.

One of the possemen, Doud Harriman, a brave-enough fellow and no fool, thought to advise his chief.

"He'll do it, Draco. Sure as hell."

"Yeah," said another man, George Lambert. "Why don't we just wait for Dansk to get back with the colored boy? He's gone after him, hasn't he?"

"He has," Ben answered for Draco.

The stillness again. Posseman talked to posseman, Draco to Fleeger, and all to all, huddling together.

"All right, Allison," the Executive announced, "we'll wait." He paused, making as though to study the cliff behind Ben. "Far as this posse's concerned, cowboy," he continued, "you still have your deal. We get the nigger kid, you go free. Jensen stays with you to guarantee it."

"Truth!" sighed Ben. "It's beautiful."

38

"You accept, then?"

"Mr. Draco," said the tall cowboy, "do I look as if the back of my head was soft? You broke our deal once."

"That's business, Allison. Don't be simple-minded."

"I ain't intending to be, believe it."

"Do you mean to say, Allison, that you were going to keep your end of the bargain, word for word?"

The dry West Texas grin flitted over Ben's dark face, lighting the pale eyes. "Oh, hell no," he protested, "but that's different. I'm a crook. It's my trade. You-all are officers of the law."

A couple of the men in the ranks sniggered audibly. But the remainder did not laugh.

All could feel a certain hidden tension of danger running high. The big cowboy was charged with murder and he looked capable of the crime. He still had his gun in hand and his revolver in his holster. Any sudden play to take him would mean death or serious injury for some of them. It was a price which, after the long night's terrible march through canyon snows, no single man of them was willing to pay or to offer.

Draco had been able to sustain their vengeance in the early going. The first defections had followed the fury he displayed at gallows tree flat. Eleven men had turned around and quit there. They had warm beds and women and, some of them, kids at home, and the idea of blood-chasing a poor damned black boy up that snow-choked canyon on tired horses—well, it wasn't a paystreak any longer for them.

The seven men here, with another three left in the canyon to cover the rear, were all that had voted to ride on with the Executive.

Now, with the Texas killer eying them and dangling the brass-framed Winchester in an all-too-familiar way, it did not strike them as uproarious to be called officers of the law. The law, of a sudden, did not seem nearly so plain as it had to them the past night on gallows tree flat.

"Cowboy," said Doud Harriman, after the long stillness, "you've still got our deal, if you want it."

39

"I've forgotten what it was," Ben answered.

"When we have the colored boy, you go free."

"So? What otherwise?"

"We will hang you both," broke in Draco.

"Reckon you will," agreed Ben. "Seeing as how I will have to kill somebody, if I don't give you the mulatto kid."

"We had a deal!" accused Fleeger, wincing as the outburst made his bandaged head hurt.

"Don't fret over it," Ben drawled. "I wasn't going to give you the boy—never. He was just my bait to get you and Mr. Draco lined up in a row."

"Lined up?" said Draco.

"I meant to kill you," said Ben. "Both of you." There was the holding of one breath. Then, softly, "I still do."

He could see the color drain from Fleeger's fat jowls, and the disfigured eye of Draco bulge outward.

And it was then that it happened, the kind of bitter thing which outlaws must always expect, but for which they are never prepared. Ben, not knowing the true count of the posse's number, could not be certain that these few men were all that Draco had with him. But he had made the lethal assumption that this *was* what was left of the original number at gallows tree flat. Draco had thought of that. The three men he had left in the outer canyon were no longer in that canyon. They had followed Draco, just as Draco had followed Dansk Jensen. The Executive was a born manhunter. Like Ben Allison, he knew a man never left his rear uncovered, but unlike Ben he did not forget that law. The three possemen, coming up quietly through the timber, had seen the drama playing out in the upper rocks of the slide. They had gotten around Ben—one to his left in the rocks, two to his right in a bristly fringe of stunted juniper scrub growing up into the rocks from the bigger timber.

Draco's bad eye was calming now.

Fleeger's jowls relaxed.

Too late, Ben read the change in their faces and body

lines. Even as he crouched to hip the Winchester and take all of them he could with him, the three trail-up possemen stood up and barked as one: "Drop it, cowboy—!"

The command came from both his flanks and from above him on both sides. He was a dead man if he moved and he did not move. Yet his foot, straining to hold its brace in the loose float-rock, betrayed him. It *did* move. And his body twisted in answer, instinctively, to regain balance.

Instantly, the flanking possemen were firing.

Ben went to his belly where he was, the rock chips flying about him and his own rifle blasting back as fast as he could throw the lever. He remembered the incessant crash and roar of many guns, as Draco and his men joined in. Then the earth seemed to explode in front of his face and he remembered nothing more.

Consciousness returned and he found himself staring up from the ground into the cold masks of two wolves panting down at him. The mists cleared still more, the wolves took on the features of men, and they were Draco and Fleeger. Then Ben Allison knew where he was. Struggling to a sitting position, back to a boulder, he found his hands had been bound behind his back. There were ten men with Draco and Fleeger now, instead of seven, and the three horses had been brought up from where Ruel Oakes had left them.

Ben shook his head, dispelling the last of the vapors and dizziness remaining from the big rock fragment which had struck and knocked him cold five minutes before. He was otherwise unwounded and, on the point of thanking a just Lord for this favor, he checked his raise. What was that Fleeger was doing with the long, coiled rope? Hard-tying it to the horn of the gray horse's saddle? The hanging horse? My God, had they caught Ruel Oakes again, while he had been out? Were they going to finish up what they started on gallows tree flat? Yes, Jesus knew, they were! For there was Fleeger shaking out the coils and throwing the rope up over the lone high limb of a lightning-riven pine not thirty feet away at the foot of the rockslide. And he

41

was coming back up toward Ben and the possemen, bringing the free end of the rope. The tall cowboy saw the noose, then, and looked about him, to the utmost craning of his stiffened neck, for sight of where they were holding poor Ruel Oakes.

But they were not holding the mulatto boy and they were not holding the rope for Ruel Oakes.

They were closing in, coming to stand close in on Ben Allison. Draco was saying in his rattler-button buzz of a voice, "Get up and walk to it like a man, you Texas scum!" And Ben was tottering unsteadily to his feet, knowing now for whom they had rigged the gray horse and doing his level best to force himself not to give them so much as a tremble or stumble or one eye-stab of fear. He managed it, too, up to the moment he saw the gunnysack in Fleeger's hand, waiting for him as it had waited for Ruel Oakes.

"No, by Christ," he said quietly, "you ain't haltering me with that. I'll look it in the eye."

One of the men—it was Doud Harriman—reached out and touched his arm. "All right," he said. "There'll be no sack." Then, dropping the hand, he said, "Two of us are against this, but we can't stop them. We tried."

"Sure," said Ben, "I know."

"No, you don't," said Harriman. "By our law, you must hang. The Alder Gulch Committee gave you the word. You were marked, aside from interfering with the colored boy's sentence. Draco planned to hang you all along. It was the law, he said. Our law."

Ben Allison said no more.

Fleeger was opening the noose to put it over his head. A gross, stout man waddled from the posse to take over this matter of adjustment. It was August Wendler, the hangman of Canyon Creek, the "rope man," as such individuals were known among the stranglers.

"You're a brave fellow," the hangman told Ben. "I will tell you something: If you don't move your head, the knot won't hurt you. When the horse jumps, let

42

yourself fall to the ground. The double jerk will snap your neck. You won't feel anything."

Ben licked dry lips.

He was going to die. The vigilantes were going to stretch him, and there wasn't one damned thing he could do to stop them.

He felt the cold grip his belly and crawl out of it, up into his chest. There was ice around his heart. His lungs would not fill. Fear had him frozen, but he would not show it. He was Comanche enough to face them down—or pray to God, and old Kadih, as well, that he was.

"Anything to say?" said the flat voice of the Executive. "Any last request within our giving?"

Ben nodded.

"Yes," he said. "Turn the little Injun horse loose. Leave him run to Texas and to home."

"That's all?"

"Yep."

"No word for kin?" It was Doud Harriman, the conscience of a fearful man stirring hard. "No one you want notified? I will promise you to carry out your wishes. You can have that peace."

"Ain't no kin," said the tall cowboy. "They're all gone, saving for my Injun folks. I wouldn't care for them to know." He winked at Harriman, and said, low-voiced, "Comanches don't think you can get to the Big Pasture on a rope."

The Canyon Creek man turned away.

"By God, Draco," he told the posse leader, white-faced, "this isn't right."

"It's the law," said the other. "Set the noose."

Hangman Wendler stood on a rock to reach high enough to drop the opened noose about Ben Allison's head. The knot for some reason would not slide freely and the rope man cursed at it. In the slight pause, Ben heard the rocks trickle and slide under the booted strides of Fleeger, as he went over to the gray, popping his quirt and whistling through his gapped teeth.

"Ready with the horse?" said Draco.

"Ready," answered Fleeger.

"You set with the rope, Wendler?"

"In a minute, in a minute. It doesn't want to take up. Ah! There."

They were the last words on earth for Hangman Wendler.

His own executioner did not use a rope. He was neither a vigilante of Montana nor any other territory.

His sword was a bullet, its vengeance as terrible and swift as the eyes of black glory could guide it. August Wendler never saw the face which held those avenging eyes, but he would have known it anywhere.

It was the face of the speckled nigger.

Ruel Oakes.

And the blunt .44-caliber bullet, fired from up on the mountain through the brand-new rifle of the Executive by the mulatto boy, struck the hangman in the throat, and he died gargling for mercy in a tongue and language no vigilante of Montana understood.

Before the stunned possemen could react to the bloody death of their own executioner, Ben Allison had shrugged away the still-untightened noose and was running, hands bound behind his back, in awkward, straining leaps up the rockslide toward the spiderweb trail. As he fled, Ruel Oakes, who had seized the Winchester from his captor, Dansk Jensen, emptied the remainder of its magazine into the scrambling Canyon Creek posse.

Ben gained the blunt-turn ledge, and life for another hour, by reason of this covering fire and the fact that the posse had laid aside their long weapons to aid in the hanging. By the time the committeemen got to their carelessly deposited rifles, Ben and the mulatto boy, with Dansk Jensen, were gone around the flank of the cliff.

On the far side, the blacksmith exchanged swift looks with the two desperate fugitives. Then, without a word, he took out his stock knife and cut Ben free. Handing the blade to Ruel Oakes, he only muttered soberly, "Every boy should have a good knife."

Then he was gone back around the turn, shouting to

44

his friends that it was he, Blacksmith Jensen, coming down unharmed and all right. "Hold your fire!" he bellowed. "They've got clean away!"

On their side of the cliff, Ruel Oakes and big Ben Allison thanked him silently for the kindness of the bit of time his lie would buy them.

Time enough, that is, to take their choice of the Canyon Creek posse and its rattlesnake leader, or old Ephraim in the bear cave up above.

The boy caught the scent of fear in Ben's hesitating looks in both directions.

His thin brown hand touched Ben's arm.

"You told me once not to be afeered," he said. "I'm turning the favor back on you. Come on."

"Up there!"

"As ever could be, Mr. Ben. There's light up yonder. Freedom light."

Ben seized him hard, told him to steady down, quit talking crazy. But the mulatto youth was not rambling wild; he was breathing freedom wind. "I seen it!" he cried. "Light at the hind end of the cave—way in yonder past the bear!"

"My God," said Ben. "A trail clean through to the rim? It can't be!"

"It's *got* to be," said Ruel Oakes.

And Ben read his eyes, and nodded, and said, yes, it did. And the two ran together up toward old Eph, and whatever lay beyond him.

11

Ruel Oakes and Ben Allison rested briefly in the same place where Dansk Jensen had taken pause in his pursuit of the mulatto youth. Breathing hard from the climb, they surveyed the den of the grizzly. There was no sound now, and no motion in the cave. Had the great bear come out? Had he gone on through the cavern, as Ruel insisted he could have done, due to the "light at the end of the tunnel"? Or was he, as seemed most likely to Ben, still in there?

In view of the latter probability, the lanky cowboy weighed their armament.

It consisted of one empty Winchester and one five-inch stockman's knife.

What of pursuit from below?

Well, Draco would never give up. Just as surely, the blacksmith would tell his fellow possemen about the bear. Dansk was a kind-hearted man, one who would not permit his friends to go unwarned against an aroused grizzly on a high ledge. Whether he would also advise Draco of the fugitives being out of ammunition for their Winchester was another guess. Crouching in the rocks eighty feet from the bear's retreat, Ben could not decide the question. To test an already stirred-up grizzly was the same as suicide. Yet to wait for Draco and the stranglers was an even more certain guarantee of death.

It did not matter whether the vigilantes came up after them, now, and shot them off the ledge from below—where they had a clear field of fire up at Ben and the boy—or whether they waited for them to die of hunger and exposure up on the ledge.

Either way, the Vigilantes of Montana would win.

And Ben Allison, like Ruel Oakes had decided before him, would rather die on his own terms a hundred times than once at the end of a vigilante rope.

But my God! To go up at that bear with a stock knife and an empty rifle!

"Come along on, Mr. Ben," urged the boy. "We don't go now, maybe they cotch us again."

"No, Ruel, they ain't ever going to do that again."

"You told me that afore."

"I know. It's different now. You've kilt a man."

"You sure, Mr. Ben?"

"Struck down as by the lightning of the Lord, boy. You couldn't have kilt him no deader had you pole-axed him and hung the carcass for the winter." Ben eyed him dubiously. "You try to make that shot, Ruel?"

"No sir," said the mulatto boy. "I just shet my eyes and squoze the trigger."

"You surely squoze it good."

The talk died away. The Negro boy, having truly killed a man now, that is, shot him down before ten adult white witnesses, friendly and unfriendly, all of Ben Allison's previous plans for justice and fair play had died with the fat body of Hangman Wendler. Even if Kadih sent them some kind of an Indian miracle to get them past old Ephraim, Ben and Ruel were in it up to their long hair from here on. Ben had become an accomplice to murder and might be a murderer plain and full. He did not know. Two of the flanking posse-men had been hit by his return fire, one of them seriously. If the badly hurt man died, it wouldn't be a question any longer of Ben and the boy having a decent plea of innocent to the charges, and gambling on the good hearts of the miners and the good legal services of Ben's friend, lawyer Esau Lazarus, up at Alder Gulch, to return verdicts of not guilty. That chance was long gone, should the man go under. The posse would never report the truth that the man had gotten hit in a gunfire fight started by the vigilantes. It wouldn't be murder that way.

Damn!

47

Well, it really didn't matter.

Ben had kicked away his own good case by running with Ruel Oakes after the Wendler shooting. The price was on his head anywhere in Montana. He had no more chance than the mulatto boy. Unless—

"What you mumbling about?" the boy asked him, interrupting his thoughts. Unknowingly, Ben had begun to frame those thoughts aloud and to himself, the old owlhoot habbit of arguing his next move with himself.

"I was thinking of us, boy," he said.

"We got to go," repeated Ruel Oakes. "Them stranglers comes round that blind turn down yonder, it's going to be like shooting carp in a hog waller, knocking us offen this-here ledge."

"Well spoke." grudged Ben. "It does seem a mite drafty here. Ain't enough cover to blanket a bedbug. But, oh man! I purely quiver at the idee of bucking that damn bear in his own boodwar."

"We ain't no choice."

"I dunno, Ruel. I believe I'd druther be shot than gummed to death. You ever get bit by a bear?"

"No sir. Did you?"

"Sure did."

"Did it hurt?"

"Hurt, hell! It kilt me."

"How come you're still walking about?"

"Ain't had time to lay down and be covered up yet. They been awaiting a year and a half down yonder to San Saba, Texas, for me to come home so's they could hold the funeral."

Ruel Oakes looked at him for a frowning moment, then grinned. It was the first time Ben had seen him smile. The mulatto boy nodded and said, "All right, Mr. Ben. I'm right sorry to hear you done passed on. Hallelujah!"

"Amen, brother!" said Ben, and they both laughed out loud, before suddenly remembering the bear.

"Shhh! For Christ's sake," whispered Ben.

"Amen," murmured Ruel Oakes.

It was as if in reply to the sentiment that a rifle shot

48

cracked from below and lead splashed the cliff wall a foot from the boy's head. Ben and Ruel went flat, but the small rock of their lofty ledge would not cover them and more lead now splattered and whined off the ledge. Beneath the rock dust and splinters of flying lead, they could see Draco and Fleeger and three of the possemen kneeling down at the blind turn. Their time, if any at all remained to them, was numbered by each screeching near-miss of the heavy .44-caliber slugs ricochetting from trail rock and cliff wall like hornets from a broken nest.

Ben yelled over to Ruel Oakes, cupping his hands to be heard above the crashing of the guns. "Last one to the bear cave's a nigger baby!" he shouted, and leaped up and ran, bent double, up the trail. Ruel almost ran up Ben's back following him. And the rifle fire of the vigilance committee bit into every footprint that they left in the rock dust of the spiderweb trail.

At the cave they both dove in behind the larger boulders there, and were safe.

For ten seconds.

They had not begun to get back breath from the wild dash when the occupant within the cliff behind them roused up from his winter's couch with a cough and a grunt and a rumbling of the chest which set every hair on Ben and the boy's neck napes standing straight on end. They not only heard the growling but the actual scrape of the great bear's six-inch claws rattling on the rock floor of the den, and any doubt of the grizzly's intent this time was dissolved.

Run sheep run, ready or not.

Old Ephraim was coming out.

12

Ben Allison was a man of the wilderness and of the wild. He knew animals, as he knew men—from life-and-death experience. The great bear, called old Ephraim by the pioneers in that grizzly country, was keen of scent but uncertain of sight. It was the one weakness the half-ton brute exhibited, and it entered Ben's mind as naturally as the question of life survival. The pale eyes swept the surroundings of the denning cavern in the instant of the bear's rumbling within. If there were any place to go, Ben intended that Ruel Oakes and himself would be long gone in its direction.

The only thing he saw was a lone snaggle of a canyon pine growing from a tiny ledge directly above the cave's mouth. Not waiting to discuss his intent, the tall man crouched, ran, and sprang upward, seizing the pine's lowest branch. Hanging there, he put down a hand for his companion.

Ruel Oakes needed no second invitation. He thought the cowboy had abandoned him to save himself one more time. Now, seeing differently, he leaped for Ben's hand and was hauled up to the shelf-sized ledge the next moment, where both fugitives tried at the same time to disappear behind the six-inch trunk of the dwarfed pine tree. In happier circumstances, it would have brought a laugh or some wry comment from Ben. As it was, he hissed angrily in the boy's ear for him to "quit shoving, for Christ's sake," and to stay utterly still—"don't even blink"—when the bear rushed out.

The grizzly exited the cliff den at that moment and the mulatto youth froze to the tree; Ben did the same

50

thing. Their retreat was not eight feet above the bear, a distance he could have reached by simply rearing upright and sweeping with his tremendous paws.

That was not the gamble.

The only hope for life was that old Eph would not look upward and, if he did, that their motionlessness, even so close, would not attract his dim vision.

The bear, as a matter of fact, had noted movement of some sort outside his den. He came out in a charging trot—head swinging, breath exploding into the air like gunshots. It was his very eagerness that carried him well away from the cliff's base, out into the boulders which half-mooned the rocky "front porch" of the grizzly's winter retreat. He came to a rearing halt, head still swinging to read the wind, some thirty feet from Ben and the boy.

Kadih, the Comanche god of Ben's Kwahadi grandmother, or some closer lord of air and earth, chose to take a hand in the affair at this tenuous moment.

The wind which the bear was sniffing changed from gusting cross-canyon currents to a steady draft from down the spiderweb trail. To the blurred images of Ben and the boy's bodies and limbs scrambling outside the opening of his home, the scents now coming to the grizzly's nostrils added up to the most hateful message in nature—man.

Not man on a ledge thirty feet behind him, but man on down the trail. Old Ephraim seemed to Ben and Ruel Oakes to grow another foot upward upon his hind legs as the sign of the enemy tainted his keen nose. The great bear, an enormous black-and-silver-maned old fellow, began to whine deep in his throat. It sounded to the boy, Ruel, exactly as some anxious and doubtful dog which, cornered, did not know what to do—bite or run. Ruel experienced vast and quick relief, thinking the bear much less fierce from this whimpering sound of uncertainty. To Ben, the sign was the opposite. The only thing worse than being in front of a grizzly which might charge was to be behind one which might not.

If that bear turned now back toward Ben and the mulatto boy, rather than advancing on Draco and his manhunters moving up from below, all hell would be let loose upon the cliffside.

Moreover, Ben's desperate plan held more than the life's leap for the pinetree ledge. It did, anyway, from the very instant that old Eph went to whining, instead of grunting and coughing the charge noises.

He put his lips an inch from the nearest ear of Ruel Oakes and mouthed the order, "Come on, boy, drop when I do!" Not waiting for the lad's agreement and not trusting the latter to make one, he grabbed Ruel's wrist and dropped from ledge to cave-mouth porch, the weight of his lanky body taking the youth with him. They made a natural and considerable double thud and the grizzly spooked around in response to it, weak eyes squinting. In the fraction of this hesitation, Ben dragged Ruel Oakes on the run with him into the den itself. He was expecting to see the daylight at the far end of the cavern which Ruel had told him of, but he did not see it. In panic, he opened and closed his eyes to the blackness of the inner pit.

It was bat-dark; he could see nothing.

But he could hear something; the whining, scuffling eagerness of the great bear scrambling to get back up to his winter nest, to ferret out, like lemmings or mice from beneath a rotten log, these audacious strange things which had invaded his slumber.

"Jesus God, boy!" Ben hissed. "Where is your goddamn light at the end of the tunnel?"

"Thisaway!" cried the boy, leaping to his left, Ben's big hand still imprisoning his wrist. The cowboy followed three lurching steps, then, far ahead and seeming no larger than the hole of a badger under a stump, he did see a muted glow of what might be light. In that precise instant, the bigger hole of the cave's mouth was blotted out of all illumination. The bear was in the mountain with them.

Ben, in the blackness, scooped the cave's floor with a free hand, and found a cannonball-sized rock. He threw it at the inky place where the bear should be, and struck grizzly gold—the very point of old Eph's sensitive snout. The distraction was a thing of no real

52

substance. But a big rock on the end of the nose is enough to make even a big bear blink, and old Ephraim roared his indignation. He even reared up in his hurt to seize his nose with both vast paws. The reaction banged his thick skull into the roof of the cavern with a thud audible to Ben and Ruel.

The thud was followed immediately by another roar from the bear and Ben freed the wrist of the mulatto boy.

"Run for it, kid!" he yelled. "Out the hole!"

The mulatto boy ran. So did the quarter-bred Comanche white man. They ran for the same hole and came to it in the same time and found it big enough for but one of them. Then the boy was already through the hole and safe outside, but Ben could not follow him. The exit was partially blocked by a boulder washed down in a recent storm. It wedged shut the spiderweb trail to the big cowboy, and trapped him facing the bear.

"The knife!" he yelled. "Gimme the knife!"

"Here!" Ruel shouted back from outside and passed in the weapon.

Ben seized the puny blade, and whirled to meet the enraged grizzly. "Keep on a'going!" he ordered Ruel Oakes, forcing his own body back into the exit hole, all he might do to protect it from the great bear. "I cain't hold him long in here!"

The brute, almost upon him, suddenly halted as the wedging of the man's body into the rear exit hole cut off the light in the back of the cavern. In the pulse-thickening instant while the bear woofed and snuffled whiningly to relocate its prey by scent, Ben saw the great form outlined faintly by the dim light from the front of the cave. Striking with all his force, Ben drove the steel into the bear. Rearing up, the giant animal clawed at the knife wound.

"Run, boy!" Ben yelled. "Run for your life!"

He heard a muffled reply from Ruel Oakes, then a sound as though of scuffling retreat on up the spider-web trail in obedience to his order. Then the bear was back again.

For three minutes the tall man fought a duel in

which his own death had to be the inevitable prize. Because his entire body, except for head and knife arm, was sheathed in the rock of the rear exit hole, the grizzly could not immediately sunder him with its great blunt claws or yellow fangs. There was a suspended segment of time when the bear feinted with both paw and fang, puzzling the matter of getting at the trapped human without again drawing the surprising hurt of the knife.

For his part Ben, grateful that the mulatto boy had at least a chance for his own freedom, devoted the final shred of strength, wilderness knowledge, desperate prayer, and raw courage to the fearful problem of fending off one thousand pounds of snarling grizzly bear with a five-inch stock knife. He could smell the fetid body odor of hibernation, hear the chomp of the gnashing fangs, feel the graze of the mighty forepaws— paws which could, with an ursine shrug, uproot a sapling or overturn a thirty-foot downed log. He was drenched with the foul slobber the great beast emitted in its fury to get at him, its lips peeled back over bared fangs. The reaching jaws, agape with power to crush a cow skull or buffalo spine or shatter a human pelvis at one closure, slashed and yawned at him. His puny arm, clawed only with a single five-inch, and fragile, steel talon, countered in silent doomed skill. It was a fight to the death now and all reasons for the effort to live were lost in the blood haze of a combat elemental and ancient, when hairier men than Ben Allison fought beasts as awesome with knives of flint from similar caves in the far dawn of human will and determination.

And, for that unknown three minutes, Ben held off the dark one who was called old Ephraim.

He had been taught the fighting of the naked steel as a boy with his grandmother's Water Horse band of Kwahadi Comanche. No less a warrior than the father of Quanah Parker had been his teacher and, unlike most white men who feared steel, Ben understood it and cherished it like a brother.

The enraged bear seeking now to dig him from his

54

rocky cocoon took full-bleeding wounds in eight or ten places before rearing back on mighty haunches to reorder his campaign to root out the white grub.

In the fleeting quiet of Ephraim's pause, Ben heard a sound which returned hope to his heart and power to his arm.

Scrape, grunt, curse, scrape, heave, grunt, scrape, curse again, and heave once more. Great God, Ruel Oakes was still out there! He had not fled on Ben's order, but had only gone to fetch a digging lever and return to scratch and scrape from his side, while the bear raged from the inner cave. "Goddamnit, boy!" Ben shouted. "I done told you to shuck out!"

"I almost got it!" the youth shouted back. "She's a'coming!"

The bear came back at Ben then and he fought the next minute as he had the first two, knowing he could not win, but refusing to quit, regardless of the consequences.

Time and luck, the two great determiners of man's life, ran together for Ben Allison as his third and last minute of defense ran out against the grizzly.

Just as a grazing blow from the bear's paw struck him in the head, Ben felt the earth and rock give way behind him. The hands of Ruel Oakes seized his feet and tugged mightily and Ben, with a final surge of his entire body, forced himself once more backward into the narrow exit hole. This time, he came out of its killing clutch, Ruel falling on top of him as he burst sprawling out of the exit. Both were raked hard by the great paw of old Ephraim, reaching out as far as the animal might force it, from the hole where its prey had just been snatched away. The blow sent Ben and the mulatto youth cartwheeling and scrambling another ten feet safely away. The only thing which followed them from the grizzly's den was the rumbling of old Eph's cheated growl. Even that sounded to the scraped and bruised pair as though the huge silvertip were grudging them a salute for their absolute gall in defeating him.

Ben sat up and dusted himself off. Folding the stock knife, their sole remaining weapon, having dropped the Executive's Winchester to leap for the pinetree ledge outside the cave, he returned it to his ripped pocket. With that, he turned and took his first look at where the spiderweb trail ran on up to the canyon rim and the freedom Ruel had talked of.

The trouble was the trail did not run very far.

Not fifteen feet from its exit of the bear cave, the spiderweb trail ended as abruptly as a dynamited road. It had been sheered off by the same avalanche which had brought down the obstructing boulder at the cave's rear opening. Another forty or fifty feet beyond this fearful gap, it resumed and did run on up to the rim in an incline as wide and straightaway as a man-built bridge.

Ben's victory grin became as extinct as old Ephraim's cave-bear ancestors, but he himself was inextinguishable.

"Well," he drawled, pointing out the fatal gap to Ruel Oakes, "as you can see purely see, you was right. Here we are, flat on our asses in the middle of an eighteen-inch goat track which peters out into bald cliff half-a-weak-spit, yonder. Yes sir, you was surely and forever correct."

"Gawd Jesus," moaned the youngster, gazing out over the sickening drop which ended the spiderweb trail. Then, recovering, he inched back toward Ben and squinted up at him. "What you mean I was right?"

"Why, cain't you see?" Ben explained. "We're free. I got to confess it, you're a genius, boy. All we got to do is jump and spread our wings."

13

"I'm powerful sorry, Mr. Ben," said the boy, huddling back against the cliff.

"That's all right, *Mr. Ruel*," grinned Ben, feeling about as funny as a broken hand but not wanting the mulatto lad to know it. "It ain't like we might not luck out yet. Who knows, boy? The bear might be so thorough woke up he'll head down the mountain to find a better hole."

There was a scraping sound behind Ben, as he spoke, and his companion's eyes widened. "I don't think so, Mr. Ben," said the boy. "But you're right, just like me. He's thorough woke up."

Ben reluctantly looked around. "Oh, Jesus," he sighed. "Eph, ain't you got nothing better to do?"

The grizzly only grunted and squealed like some giant pig intent on rooting up acorns. But he was excavating loose rock and decomposed granite and ripping away entire chunks of the cave floor on his side of the exit hole. And he wasn't after acorns.

"We may have to do it, after all," said Ruel Oakes, squeezing yet farther away from the exit and the flying bear claws.

"Huh?" Ben asked, puzzled. "Do what?"

"Jump," answered the boy in a small voice.

"Ah!" said Ben. "One for the nigger boy." He put out a long arm, patted the other on the head. "Mr. Ruel," he grinned, "I'm beginning to cotton to your style. You ain't worth a damn, but I'll be dogged iffen I don't let you go first." He looked around, just as the bear's huge head thrust itself out of the enlarged hole to eye them both and cough out a mouthful of slobber. "Why, hello," Ben said, greeting the brute. "Where you been all winter?" He reached for the stick Ruel had used to dig away the boulder. With a quick blow, he hit the great bear squarely across its wrinkled and dirty nose. Ephraim gaped, jaws full wide, inhaled, sneezed mightily, withdrew head back into cave. In a moment the vast claws reappeared in their fierce digging away to open up the hole, which now was already large enough for them to see the baleful and tiny eyes of the aroused grizzly behind the working paws. "Go ahead on, partner," Ben Allison said to Ruel Oakes. "Time has come to jump. Flap hard and don't look down."

"I ain't ready yet," whispered the mulatto boy, shivering again as he looked at the drop-off beneath them. "You go ahead."

Ben and the boy looked at one another. Eight feet away, the great bear had its head and one thick forelimb out of the hole. He was about through to them. With a feeling he did not argue, the big cowboy swept the Negro youth close to his side, comforting him with the circle of his arm. "Get behind me, boy," he ordered, "and this time do what you're told." Ruel nodded and scuttled against the cliff. Ben opened blacksmith Jensen's knife. "Eph," he said, "gimme your paw."

As though hearing him, the reaching forefoot of the grizzly groped toward the cowboy. Ben, timing his reply to the friendly gesture, drove the knifeblade into the flesh of the brute's mammoth palm. Roaring, the huge animal bit in a fury at the weapon, stuck to its guard in the bones and sinews of the tender paw. At the first snap of foaming jaws, the haft of the weapon splintered, leaving only a steel tang too small for the bear to grasp in its teeth. Crying with hurt and rage, the grizzly pulled back into its lair. Inside, they could hear him moaning; it sounded almost human.

"I wouldn't care," said Ben Allison grimly, "to meet up with him just now. We'd best pray to Jesus the blade takes his mind off us." Unconsciously, he edged closer to Ruel Oakes. "Meanwhile," he amended, "we had best just pray—straight. You got any Bible-learning, boy?"

The mulatto drifter nodded. The homeliness of his freckled features took on a sudden new light. "All the learning I ever did have was from my mama's Bible," he told the big Texan. "What part you want?"

Ben's answering nod was direct.

"How about the Green Pastures part?" he said. "It sort of gets a man ready either way."

Ruel Oakes moved his eyes instinctively to where the great bear groaned and mauled about within the cave. It seemed as though he hesitated to start any prayer that worked both ways. He was renewed in his spirit, however, by the reappearance of the grizzly's pig-small eyes in the exit hole, and the resumed scraping of its claws.

"The Lord is my Shepherd, I shalt not want. He leadeth me to lay down whar——" he began, then broke off.

Ben, too, became strainingly alert. Both comrades of the ledge bent their ears hard caveward. Could they possibly have heard what they thought they had heard?

The great bear also fell into softly grunting motionlessness. The stubs of its ears twisted flat to the heavy skull. He strained as intently as the two humans to recatch the outer cliff sounds which had brought Ruel Oakes and Ben Allison to a last-hope attention.

There it came again—unmistakable as it was unbelievable.

Draco and his picked riflemen were coming up outside the grizzly's den. They were calling back and forth among themselves, cautioning each other to be wary of the human prey they sought but, amazingly, not yet aware of the fact that they were walking up on old Ephraim.

"God Amighty," breathed Ben. "You're some hard prayer, Ruel Oakes!"

The boy did not answer. He did not comprehend, as his companion did, the singular meaning of the posse's failure to pick up the bear sign. He did not understand,

59

as Ben did, that it was the stranglers' eagerness for the capture of Ruel Oakes that was leading them, unwarned, into the great bear's wounded anger.

"I want that nigra alive!" they heard Draco command in the last minute. "Shoot the other, if you must."

In that same final minute they heard one of the men belatedly call out to his leader, "Hold on, *patron*. I've spotted bear sign. Watch it, *mes amis*. Stay back."

"Nonsense, you fools!" cried Draco. "No bear is going to stay around all this rifle fire and racket we've made getting up here. Let's go, men. Follow me."

In that moment, before the men could act, the grizzly erupted ragingly from the den. By a miracle, the bear bowled over Draco in its first heedless fury to be at the human intruders it heard and smelled. The posse leader's very nearness to the den's mouth saved his life. He came up out of the detritus of the den's outer level none the worse but for some deep gouges and a mouth clogged with rock dust. Not so fortunate were his two close followers. The one, Edward Dobbs, was seized in the bear's up-reared embrace, crushed to the hairy breast, and his skull bitten into a greasy gray-and-white-sharded pulp of brain and bone splinters, in a single gaping bite. The second man, Thomas Clarke, was struck by two swipes of the gigantic paws and nearly torn in two. But his sufferings were no more prolonged than those of the headless Dobbs. The force of the bear's blows sent Clarke's body gyrating down the trail and over its edge. Thomas Clarke lived only as long as the thin fading of his scream far below. He was dead when he struck the bottom rocks of the sightless depths.

Rearing upright, the grizzly turned upon the remaining three of his enemies.

These were Selkirk Johnson, Frenchy Burloign, and W. T. Harris, all respected members of the mining community of Canyon Creek. Burloign was a French Canadian, with some Cree Indian blood, and no stranger to the mountain West. It was he who had seen the bear sign and backed off, taking Harris and Johnson with him. Now it seemed old Eph would kill them, as he had Dobbs and Clarke.

It was not to be; the strings of great bears run out as commonly as those of small men.

Behind the towering grizzly, Draco had recovered his footing and his sawed-off manhunting ten-gauge shotgun. A man of absolute fearlessness, the Executive walked into the very shadow of the huge grizzly to plant the charges from both barrels into the beast's great body at powder-burning range. The chilled-iron Double OO buck pellets literally tore the bear apart. He fell slowly like a forest giant, toppling at last with a crash of ledge-trembling weight. In the moment of his downing, Draco slipped past him and ordered his men to "get down the trail," if they preferred. He himself was going to check out the cavern.

"I didn't come up here to kill bears," he advised his followers. "They've got to be in there."

There was a silence upon the mountainside.

"Let them be," said Burloign. "The bear has got them. God's name!"

Draco did not answer him, but turned and went back up to the cavern's mouth. "Allison," he called. "It's no use. Come out."

The wind drafted up the canyon while the Executive waited and, down the trail from him, his men did likewise. In the stillness one of them—it was Burloign—moved up to flank his leader. Draco looked around at him. There was no greeting, no gesture, even, of appreciation.

Across the blackness of the inner cave, Ben and the mulatto boy huddled outside the exit hole. They had heard it all in the killing of old Ephraim, including Draco's challenge to Ben to come out. Neither the tall white outlaw nor the small colored outcast answered that challenge. They had thought, for one wild moment of hope, that the grizzly's attack on the possemen had been the answer to Ruel Oakes' prayers.

Now they knew better.

Death again was calling upon them to come forth, to surrender to him, to die for their sins.

61

And now they did not have even blacksmith Jensen's little knife for a weapon of defense—or defiance.

"Coming in," announced the dry voice of the posse leader.

In that final second, Ben had the presence of mind to throw his body into the exit hole, blocking its light. When Draco entered the cave and made his own light with flaring sulphur matches lit in smoky sequence, he saw nothing but the place where Ephraim slept and the rocks and rubble that were the skirts of the old king-bear's couch.

The last match burned his fingers and he cursed and dropped its blackened stick, bent, and went out of the cavern and down to his waiting men.

"Nothing up there," he said. "No sign of them."

Frenchy Burloign nodded. "Sure, *patron;* they went over the edge, like I told you."

"Certain sure," confirmed Selkirk Johnson, glancing into the awesome depths of the cleft. "We damned near went over ourselves, every one of us."

"Let's get out of here," murmured the last man, Harris. "This place gives me the fantods."

"All right," nodded Draco, "I am content."

He turned without further word and led the way below. The others followed, intent on footing and pace, aware now that death did indeed await those who used the careless foot or wrong placement of weight on the high trail.

It was half an hour before they rounded the blind turn to come in sight of their fellows who had stayed upon the bench. When they did, all but Draco broke into a sliding, falling haste to be down the last, easy part of the spiderweb trail and away from the lonely hidden bench where only disaster had come to them and their hangman. The body of Edward Dobbs, brought down with them, was strapped on the dead man's horse. No effort was made to go into the bottom of the deep cleft in search of Thomas Clarke's near-sundered corpse. The horses of Draco and Jensen being reclaimed, the posse went down across the bench toward the main canyon. The posse leader and the town blacksmith did not ride their recovered mounts; these honors were reserved for the seriously injured posseman shot by Ben Allison, and for his fellow, shot by Ruel Oakes —hangman Wendler, whose gross bulk was sacked, stone dead, over the saddle of Dansk Jensen's bay.

Three men dead, a fourth who might yet die.

But it was to the Executive a satisfactory bargain.

With the payment of those lives of good men, he had purchased whatever it was that he must have.

He was, as he had attested, content.

Swiftly, the little cavalcade came to the bench top-out. As swiftly, it went over the topping place, down and out the false door, into the outer canyon.

Within an hour, it was as though no human had come to Poo Cat's place, nor to great Ephraim's high lair upon the spiderweb ledge.

14

After a long, suspenseful wait, Ben and Ruel crawled to the cave's entrance. Peering out, they saw the motionless form of old Ephraim. Feeling the power of the brave animal even in death, they went outside and stood beside the giant bear. Ben touched the fingertips of his left hand to his forehead in the Plains Indian salute of final respect for the fallen enemy. Ruel kneeled down by the huge head and gently closed the open-staring, pain-filled eyes. It was a kind thing to do and Ben's Comanche blood appreciated it. When the boy stood up, he and the tall man shared a new closeness.

"Time to go," said Ben. "It's all done here."

They set out down the spiderweb trail and reaching the bench, they found it seemingly deserted. They went on cautiously through the timber to the rocks at the head of the drop-off trail. Here, they heard nothing from the outer canyon and Ben showed his first genuine relaxation. "Quiet down yonder," he nodded to the boy. "Good sign."

Straightening, the tall outlaw looked for a last time over the sunlit beauty of the bench—over the small meadow, the dark stand of conifers, the rearing cliffs above. Again, he nodded, this time to himself.

Good-bye old Ephraim. Good-bye Poo Cat's place. Good-bye magpies. Good-bye Montana Territory. Good-bye stranglers of Canyon Creek. Ben Allison was gone from there.

"Let's ramble," he said to the mulatto youth, at the same time warning him with a wave. "Don't slide no rocks underfoot, nor talk no more. We still ain't made the Wyoming line."

They went crouchingly down the steep track into the outer canyon. It was as empty of vigilante horsemen as the upper bench. Ben let out long-held breath. As a matter of good feeling, he grinned and said to Ruel Oakes, "Well, whichaway you vote for?" But never really doubting the choice of the freckled Negro lad. But the youngster only frowned and shook his head and turned stubborn.

"I didn't do it," he announced unexpectedly.

Ben was not prepared for the detour. "What the hell is that supposed to mean?" he demanded sharply.

"I never kilt the lady and I want to go back."

"By Christ, you cain't go back. You've truly kilt a man since then. It's all changed now."

"No sir, it ain't, Mr. Ben. It was you said it, not me. We got to go back. Remember?"

"Oh, Jesus, sure I remember," Ben groaned. "But what I said then don't count no more. They think me and you are dead now. That puts us to running free, boy. Don't you understand that? Hell!" he cried, his arm sweeping up the canyon toward Wyoming. "We *are* free. We don't need to run no more, just walk."

Ruel Oakes did not budge.

"No sir, we ain't free," he denied quietly. "We ain't

64

never free so long as they say we done what we didn't
do. Ain't that what you said, Mr. Ben?"

The tall cowboy took a long time with his answer.

He thought about who he was, and where he was,
and who and what Ruel Oakes was. He added it up
and counted the sum in his head half a dozen times
and still could not get it to come out anything better
than one plus one. Or, as the vigilantes counted it—
two.

Two, that was, for the sycamore tree.

"Mr. Ben," queried the anxious voice of Ruel Oakes.
"You done fell asleep?"

Ben shook away the spell of the stranglers.

"No, hell no, boy," he protested. "Wish I had, sort
of. That way I could just be waking up and finding out
you wasn't there at all. The way that it is, though, you
ain't no more broke down in your head than I am, and
I will prove it to you, right now."

He stepped back and made the Indian-respect sign
toward the mulatto boy, and said in his soft Lone Star
drawl, "Mr. Ruel Oakes, you have done hired yourself
a Texas gunfighter—soon as he gets his gun back.
Lead on."

There was a singular change in the tall cowboy and
the youth saw it. There was no easy grin behind the
south plains' drawl and an expression, half of pride,
half of fearful awe, came into the thin face of Ruel
Oakes. He really *had* hired himself a Texas gunfighter—
he knew it—gun or no gun.

The boy squared his bony shoulders, thrust out his
dirt-smudged chin. "Thank you, Mr. Gunfighter," he
said, and set out along the hoof-packed snows of the
vigilante trail to Canyon Creek, Montana.

15

The day turned off warm, settling the snow and firming it for the horses of the downward-bound posse. In excellent time, but depressed spirits, the vigilantes came again to the gallows tree flat in the main canyon. Here Draco, ostensibly to rest the scarcely lathered horses, ordered a halt. The returning cavalcade strung itself out on the sandy floor, glad enough to get down and stretch.

At this point the group, in addition to Draco and his fat sergeant, Fleeger, consisted of Dansk Jensen, Jack Spain, George Lambert, Selkirk Johnson, W. T. Harris, Frenchy Burloign, and Doud Harriman. Sacked dead over their horses were August Wendler, Edward Dobbs, and Charley Farwood, the latter dying on the trail down from wounds taken in the gunfire with Ben Allison. Jack Spain, the other wounded posseman, was in good condition. Left dead and forever lost in the awesome crevice below Ephraim's den was Thomas Clarke, recording secretary of the Canyon Creek Committee.

Four vigilantes dead: one killed by a starveling, teen-aged Negro boy from ambush; one blasted down out of a cold-deck surround by a Texas trailherd hand; two mutilated past recognition as men by an enraged bear on a high trail where no retreat was possible once the grizzly was forced to come. It was a grim accounting.

Draco exactly understood this fact. It was the true reason for the halt on the flat. An agreement must be had within the posse. The vigilante *modus operandi* demanded it. The stranglers did not make mistakes.

Mistakes were the one enemy which might undo the law which rode by night. The survivors could not reveal their flawed performance even to their fellow possemen who had abandoned the pursuit the previous night. Grimly, the Executive called the men in about him.

As they gathered reluctantly, one of their number was slower than the rest. Doud Harriman had another order of vigilante business to attend. In the bylaws of the nightriders, last requests of the doomed were honored to the letter. The Executive and his instructions to the dispirited manhunters would have to proceed without Doud Harriman, for the latter had asked the dead Texan for his final wish. He regarded it as a legal testament and, in contest, Draco's terse orders to his pet hanging jury, which had hung no one, came a limping second.

The lone posseman's interest lay with the last horse in the grim pack string of riderless and corpse-ridden animals being led on the trail by Dansk Jensen and his stout bay. As he came up to the string, the blacksmith was just swinging down off the bay to go forward and hear Draco's advice for a return to Canyon Creek. He surely saw, and as surely understood, Doud Harriman's business there. But he merely nodded to the other man and kept on plodding up the halted line of pack animals toward the meeting.

"Thanks," said Harriman softly in passing, and did what he had to do.

But he was hasty and, in getting the Texas outlaw's Comanche pony freed from the others in the string, he neglected to first remove from its saddle scabbard the tall man's Winchester, and likewise the belted holster and long-barreled .44 pistol hung about the high saddlehorn. Consequently, when the mustang spooked and got away from him prematurely, all that the good fellow might do was shout aloud—very loud, it seemed—that, damn it all, the crazy Indian horse of the dead outlaw had just plain gotten away from him! He was sorry as all get out but it was just one of those things. He had

67

intended only to free the small brute in compliance with the last request of the big Texan. And surely the others would agree to the simple honor in that. The Vigilantes of Montana were not, after all, without their traditions.

Draco, rushing in a hurried stumble to the pack string, was nicely boxed. Fury burned in his deformed eye, but reason had not departed his vengeful mind.

The others of the posse following him up through the snows of the flat were in time to see, with their leader, the bounding form of the Indian pony vanish into the rocks and brush of the main canyon, heading southward. All knew, as Draco surely did, that a mile south from where they stood, the canyon flared wide to open on a rangeland of gullies and stunt timber and high Montana grass that would hide all the Comanche mustangs in Texas.

"He's gone," said someone to no one in particular, and a wash of wordless nods cemented the pronouncement.

The Executive did not argue the company concession.

It might even be, he said, that things had worked out as they should. He understood from the Alder Gulch Committee that Allison had been part-Indian and he seemed to remember that, when an Indian died, the tribe sent his pony along with him to carry him on that last lonely trail. "Of course, we don't know about the poor nigra boy," he concluded. "Guess he will have to walk."

It was as close as Selman Draco came to humor.

Two of the men rewarded the effort with a forced grin, a third coughed and said it was getting cold again, and had they not best get on with the meeting and scatter for home?

The Executive briefly eyed them, and as briefly laid out the posse line of tracks to show Canyon Creek when they got back. The gist of the instruction was to say nothing at all, but refer all inquiries to the committee under the normal vigilante procedure.

"Said committee being me," he said. "There will be no problem. Mount up."

When they were gone, two separate visits were made to the gallows tree flat in their wake.

The first was made by a tall white man and a young mulatto boy on foot and walking fast. They were not an hour behind the posse and staying as close to it as they might, the better to know of its doings. After a time of stillness following their departure north to the mining camp, the other visitor came in. It was a wiry Texas mustang, nervous and touchy, bearing full saddle and rigging. It nosed the trampled snows of the lynching flat, quartering the boot and horseshoe marks as swiftly and intently as a hunting dog. When it had found the line of tracks it sought, the Comanche pony gave a low-throated whinny and began to trot briskly in the opposite direction to its wary return—due north toward the Canyon Creek gold diggings, following the Vigilantes of Montana.

16

The gold of Canyon Creek was in the gravel of the lower levels. The value of the claims rose or fell on their proximity to the streambed. As with all placer deposits, water was the essential. Second-level claims, where the water had to come by dug or boxed ditch, had a tenth the value of the discovery claims. At the third level where, even with ditch or flume, water came not at all in dry spells or times of heavy call upon Canyon Creek by the primary-bed-level sites, claims were, again, a fraction of the worth of even second-level strikes.

Even higher, far up on the waterless gullies, spurs

and ridges climbing from creekbed elevation hundreds of feet below, were the parched glory holes.

These were the drifts, run into the hillsides horizontally, and the shafts, sunk down vertically, dug in fevered seeking for the big vein. They were the stark labors of men who dreamed of the main lode, the source place from whence, eons gone, had come all the fine and coarse gold of the lower placers.

The dreamers cared not for the washing of the gravel, the sluicing of the sands, the grubbing in the black mud of the icy creekbottom for a show of color in the pan that would buy supplies for a week of added hell. Or a riffle-box cleanup where the dog-mean toil of a week would make a man wealthy for one night in the canvas whiskey shacks and wagonbox whorehouses of the town. They were men after the big strike, the granddaddy pocket, and they lived on their illusions and the grubstaking of other fools as great as they.

The ancestor of all the lode-finding high holes drifted or shafted into the back-country ridges was the Old Glory Mine, a maze of tunnels, air holes, stopes, galleries, and gopher runs—exploratory finger drifts—that was sole monument to the burrowing years of one man—Walter J. "Pegleg" Gates.

It was said in the town that of certain nights, when the lone wolf howled and the moon rose late beyond the bitterroots, Pegleg yet prowled and patrolled the wasted workings of a lifetime. People laughed, but they stayed away from the Old Glory. In the seasons now passed since Pegleg's disappearance, trapped, no doubt, in exploring some new lead far underground, no miner from the creeks had come to seek his body or to ferret out the secret of his lost, dry-rock bonanza.

It waited silent in the sunshine, wind-whipped in the winter cold, eleven-hundred feet above the kerosene lights of Canyon Creek on the western flank of the waterless ridge called Ghost Hill. No single man in all the camps, they said, Alder Gulch to Burro Flats, knew the mappings of the old man's catacombed mountainside. And they were right.

No man did, but a boy did.

17

Ben and Ruel Oakes came to the foot of Ghost Hill in the twilight of the brief winter day. Here, a mile outside Canyon Creek, the trail forked around the mountain—west to the diggings, east to Bozeman City. Ben nodded to his companion, pale eyes searching the gloom.

"Two things mainly make a man elect hisself a hero," he muttered. "One's whiskey, other's distance."

The mulatto youth also examined the quality of the gathering dusk. "Yeah," he said, "close up, it don't seem the same. Wisht we did have a drink."

"Well, we ain't. Likewise, we've run out of room."

"Sure enough we have. Town's just around the bend."

"What was it we was going to do?" Ben asked. "I forgot."

"Find who kilt my purty lady and yore moneyman."

"Oh, yeah," said Ben, "and bust up the stranglers."

It sounded absurd—crazy even. Both of them knew it. Oddly, it was Ruel Oakes who first put words to it.

"You want to quit, Mr. Ben?"

"I dunno. How about you, Mr. Ruel?"

The mulatto boy shivered, and pressed closer for warmth to the tall man crouching by his side in the thicket of trailside pine scrub. "I'm dreadful feered," he said.

"Me too," Ben admitted. "Likewise dreadful froze.

We got to get on up into that old mine of yours, boy."

Ruel started to reply, but time had run out on them.

Of a sudden, from the direction of the diggings, came a muttering sound of many people marching. The coming night was at once lit by the flicker of approaching illuminations. "My God," Ben said, "another posse?"

As he spoke, a considerable company on foot drew near around the bottom of Ghost Hill. It was composed of men, women, and some few children from the mining community. Heading it was a creaking wagon bearing a prisoner of some description not yet clear to the hidden watchers.

Ben did recognize the driver, though. He was one Gaskins, the man picked by the Vigilance Committee to handle the mercantile business of the man Ben was accused of having murdered and robbed out on the Bozeman Road. The big cowboy also recognized the four mounted torchbearers flanking the wagon, and his pale eyes narrowed.

"Boy," he whispered, "come close. It's them again."

Ruel Oakes stared fearfully at the four mounted marshals of the noisy foot parade: fat Fleeger, gaunt Selman Draco, the wounded Jack Spain, head tracker Frenchy Burloign—the high command of the local stranglers.

The crowd was around the bend and at the Forks now.

The standing figure in the bed of the wagon was seen to be not a man but a woman—and not just some woman.

"Jesus Gawd," murmured the mulatto boy, "it's the lady done testify I kilt her friend."

"Ah," gritted Ben, "chickens ain't the only birds comes home to roost. Doves do too."

"Huh?"

"They're running her out of town, boy. Somebody's wife done caught her working overtime, and for free."

72

The tall outlaw's assay now ran a thousand dollars to the sack. The creaking tumbrel from Canyon Creek halted opposite their hiding place, discharged Elvira Semple, and left her stranded in the crusting snows of Bozeman Fork.

Indignantly and not without some detectable pride, the unwanted lady denied the charge. The good wife of the settlement who accused her was a damned liar. The vigilantes who, in result, blue-ticketed her out of the Montana Territory were a pack of four-letter bastards whom she would return to haunt. The entire procedure was a trap set and baited by the stranglers, damn their scheming souls. They had not heard the last of Elvira June Semple nor had Canyon Creek, Montana.

Her defiance sang out on the night air with such a string of ringing, round oaths that Ben Allison could not help but admire, at least, the fighting spirit of the branded woman. Even Ruel Oakes, with every cause to hate and despise her, was affected.

"Lordy, Lordy," he said. "It ain't right. Lookit there. They really are aleaving her in the road."

They were indeed.

With a final burst of returned invective the righteous wives of the diggings departed homeward. After them, pausing only to hurl the last barrage of snowballs, sticks, and rocks at the evil angel, traipsed their wet-nosed dirty children. The men brought up the rear, plainly regretful of the whole thing. Within minutes the torchlights flickered out around Ghost Hill. Mrs. Elvira Semple stood alone in the wind and cold of the Forks. Judgment Day for her was a winter's night.

But the Semple woman, if a bit soiled, was still no cooing dove. Picking up her carpetbag, she uttered a final four-letter farewell to the retreating mob and turned resolutely to face the foot march to Wyoming. She had taken a dozen thrusting, stumbling strides when Ben and Ruel caught up with her.

"Evening, ma'am," Ben said. "You lost your way or your mind?"

Elvira Semple whirled about. She cocked the carpetbag as though to lay Ben out cold with it.

73

"Watch yourself!" she warned. "I'm the wife of the mayor of Canyon Creek."

"Just out for a little night air, missus?"

"Yes, I like these brisk evenings. Any minute now His Honor will be riding around the bend to join me."

"Yes, ma'am. Meanwhile, me and my friend would admire to chaperone you."

Ellie Semple backed away, still brandishing the carpetbag. "What friend?" she demanded. "I don't see anybody."

"It's me, Miz Semple." The soft-voiced mulatto lad stepped from behind Ben. "Remember?"

It was full dark now and she could not see the features of the speaker, but she knew that southern voice.

"You!" she gasped. "The speckled nigger!"

"Well, yes," admitted Ruel, "thank you, ma'am."

Ellie drew back the bag, full-swing. "Don't you dast touch me! You do, I'll raise a screech will bring every manjack miner in the diggings on the double run." She cast an accusing eye at Ben Allison. "I don't know who you are, mister, or what you two got in your minds. But you're a white man. You got to protect a white woman."

"White as a dove," Ben nodded. "You, I mean, not me. I'm a quarter Comanche Injun. Reckon you're in a frightful fix, true enough. Caught twixt a nigger and a redtail Injun. Why, you ain't no chanct, at all."

Cursing, she swung at him with the bag. She missed badly and fell in the freezing slush of the road. "Goddamn big lanky bowlegged sonofabitch!" she yelled, falling again as she struggled to rise. "Just wait till I get up here!"

Ben reached down and lifted her easily to her feet.

"Yes, ma'am," he said, "You're up."

The dancehall woman was breathing hard. Even in the darkness, Ben took note of the handsome rise and fall of the bust beneath the cheap cloth coat. He liked the way the rest of her moved around, too—quick and full of spring, not weak and knock-kneed like most. He just bet, too, that come daylight a man would see she had red hair and a black, flashing eye. Irish, Ben guessed, with a little Mexican or French or Spanish mixed in. He knew the breed from the Rio Grande to Canada. They were real fighters and that wasn't all they were real at.

"Ma'am," he said, taking her arm respectfully, "come on along with us. You will surely freeze to death going this Wyoming road." He hunched his back to the rising wind. "We all of us got to get in out of this cold, missus. Temperature's dropping like a shot out of a short cannon."

But again Ellie Semple pulled away.

It seemed that, to her, the deadly Montana weather was less a gamble than a hatchet-faced, long-haired squawman running with a speckled bad nigger.

"I can make it to Shafter's place, thank you," she said, tightening the threadbare coat about her. "They will take me in. Stand out of my way."

Ben could see, against the snow, the way the wrapped coat set off her hips. Mrs. Elvira Semple might be down on her hustler's luck, maybe even a little long in the tooth for her shady trade, but she still had a figure no man could ignore, nor long neglect, and Ben would remain betting that she had red hair. Every place.

"Shafter's is nine mile, missus," he said. "You'd best come along with me and the boy."

The argument was not concluded, Ruel Oakes interrupting it to warn sharply, "Rider coming in from the south. Listen."

Ben heard it immediately, for the road had frozen solid since twilight. The approaching horseman's mount made a clacking of hooves, breaking the crust-ice, that was unmistakable. Ben seized the Semple woman by the waist and deposited her over his shoulder. "Horseman's got the right of way every time," he said to Ruel. "Back into the bullpines, boy."

For whatever reason of instinct or suffocating fear,

75

Ellie Semple did not cry out and, next moment, she and the two wayfarers were hidden in the roadside scrub. Another moment and the horseman hove into view. Only it wasn't a horseman; it was just a horse.

A raunchy animal it was, as well. Sort of an admixture of Indian colors: roan paint with gaudy bay appaloosa, rump all splattered with white, tail a rat of black bristles, mane the same, white nose and four full stockings up to knees and hocks. It even came already saddled and bridled, with a Winchester rifle in scabbard and a Colt .44-caliber revolver in cartridge-belt rig slung about the high southwestern saddlehorn.

Ay de mi, as they said down on the border. Truly a horse to remember.

Remembering him, Ben Allison leaped up from the roadside cover with a startling Comanche yell of *"Wagh—!"*

Poo Cat spooked wildly, then recovered and came trotting back to whinny and nose-rub the tall man with happy mustang grunts. "Ma'am," said Ben to Elvira Semple, "leave me hoist you up on this-here horse, and no more auguring it. We got to get off this icy road and on up into the mountain."

"He means up into the Old Glory Mine, Miz Semple," explained Ruel Oakes. "You know, the one I was camped in when the stranglers tooken me."

"Oh, God," groaned the woman, "no. I'm not going up there. Not at night, not ever."

"Maybe not ever," nodded Ben, circling her waist and savoring its firm feel, "but as for right now, you're going." He lifted her to the saddle and turned to Ruel.

"Boy," he said, "lead the way; make it the back way whiles you're at it."

"All right," said Ruel doubtfully, "but you cain't get the horse into the mine thataway. There ain't room. Not no way there ain't."

"Get along," snapped Ben. "Horse is Kwahadi-bred. He can run outside with the deer." He glanced up at the settlement woman. "You all set, missus?"

76

"Oh, my God," answered Ellie Semple. "How do I know?"

"That's the spirit," Ben said. "You're a scrapper, sure enough."

"I am? Well, isn't that wonderful, you big dumb cowhand. Oh, dear God!"

For causes of inner doubt or natural release of nerves, Elvira Semple began to weep—to weep hard. Ben, unsettled by the tears, turned angrily on Ruel Oakes.

"Goddamnit, boy, get along like I told you. We ain't never going to get under cover. Move out!"

Wisely, the mulatto lad obeyed. They set out in silence, except for the sobs of their guest. In an hour they had not yet come to the rear entrance to Pegleg Gates' old mine and Ben uneasily called the halt.

"Ruel Oakes, by God," he wanted to know, "how far on around the backside of this-here mountain you taking us?"

"Only another mile," answered the boy, "least I hope so." There was a disconcerting pause. "I sure *prays* I can find that-there back way into the mine again."

"You don't find it," Ben said grimly, "you damned sure better pray."

"Lemme get my wind," pleaded the boy, and Ben nodded.

He even gave the situation one wry Texas grin.

It was worth it.

Here they were—two wanted murderers and one out-of-work mining-camp whore. A mostly white woman. A three-quarters white man. A half-white, half-nigger kid. The three outcasts of Canyon Creek. Jesus H. Christ. Somebody had better warn the poor damned done-for Vigilantes of Montana. They had no idea of the deep trouble they were in. Ruel Oakes was coming for them. Him and his big Texas gunfighter. Whee-yew! Why, if they knew that, every strangler in the territory would be running for his life. Ben sighed wearily, and lifted his dark Indian face to the snow-clouded sky above.

"Kadih," he said, calling on the old god of his grandmother's people, "you got a set of good directions for two tomfool menfolk and a redheaded hooker on their ways to Nowhere, Montana, and not even a jug of whiskey to get them there?"

The Comanche great spirit answered not. Elvira Semple's sobs had long since ceased. It began to snow again—hard. Oh, Christ, thought Ben, and left Poo Cat and the quieted woman to go forward to find Ruel Oakes. He discovered the boy huddled behind a pine stump licking snowflakes, wiping his nose, almost crying.

"Buck up," Ben said. "You'll find it."

"No sir," sniffled Ruel. "I reckon I'm plain lost."

"Plain or fancy," Ben said, "you was lost the day you was born. Trick is to find yourself. How you going to do that without you keep looking, Ruel Oakes?"

He reached the mulatto lad, who gathered himself once more and answered, "All right," and started forward again. Ten minutes along the branch creek they were following, they struck another, larger stream. Ben was laboring behind with the mustang pony and the woman when he heard ahead the muffled cry of *"Wagh!"* and then a triumphant, "Here we be! Praise the Lord. Old God, He done guide us square to it."

Ben nodded, and reached to help Poo Cat's rider down.

"Sure He did," he said aloud to the whirling snow. "Him and my little old lost nigger boy."

"What?" said the Semple woman, rousing in the saddle.

"Nothing," Ben answered proudly. "Not a damned thing you would believe, missus. Nor me neither—yesterday."

18

Ben unsaddled and turned loose Poo Cat. Joining Ruel at the creek, he looked around and said, "Where's it at?"

"Yonder," answered the boy, pointing to where the stream disappeared underground into the mountain.

"That's the hole?"

"Yes sir."

"Oh, my God," said Elvira Semple, coming up.

"It's all right, lady," Ruel assured her. "It opens up onct we get squoze past the entrance. You'll see."

Ben decided they would, for the mulatto boy did not wait for their agreement but simply wriggled into the tiny opening and was gone. "Follow me," said the big cowboy, and exhaled hard, trying to make himself as small as possible. He barely made it in, pushed from the rear by Ellie Semple, hauled on from in front by Ruel Oakes. Inside, however, the pit darkness was suddenly illuminated by a miner's candle. They saw Ruel grinning behind the candle's glow and, beyond the mulatto boy, a spacious cavern beckoning. Crawling along the narrow ledge above the foaming creek, they came to the inner room.

"Well, anyhow," sniffed Mrs. Elvira Semple, looking around, "it beats hell out of a bed in the bottom of a camp wagon."

"Yeah," Ben said, side-eying her, "maybe even out of one in a canvas-wall boodwar upstairs at the Oriental."

"You'd ought to know," answered the woman easily.

79

Ben ignored her; after all, there was a child present. "Ruel," he enthused, "you have hit paydirt."

"This here ain't even sluicebox mud to what's coming, Mr. Ben," the mulatto boy said. "Just you wait."

Little Big Canyon Creek, he told them, ran inside the mountain for a full quarter mile. Naturally, the diggings' people knew that it did this. What they didn't know was that there was a way that human beings could go with the stream into Ghost Hill. Not understanding that, they couldn't know of the vastness of the caves and tunnel-runs that nature had carved out, from where the three of them now rested to the top of the ridge above Canyon Creek.

Ben Allison was incredulous.

"You saying this-here chain of cracks and crevices runs clean up to old Pegleg's glory hole? I mean, for us to foller it up there *inside* the hill?"

"Yes sir. Easy as walking up the outside."

Pegleg Gates, the boy continued, had always known that it was this "Mother Nature's honeycomb of holes" that made his own tunnelings practical. The system drained and ventilated the entire ridge, keeping every stope, drift, run and shaft dry and airy. The knowledge of this natural boon had been the second-to-the-main-one of the Old Glory's secrets, or so the old man had privately attested.

"The *second*-to-the-main secret, eh?" Ben eyed the boy, wondering how he knew so much about Pegleg Gates. "What might you say would be the *first*-to-the-main secret?"

"I cain't tell you; I promised."

"The hell. Who you promised? Old Pegleg's ghost?"

"I cain't tell you."

"Yeah, I know," Ben nodded. "You promised."

"Yes sir."

Elvira Semple, no woman to be detained by the secrets of old mines, or old miners, interrupted wearily. "You two mind if we get on upstairs? Wherever we're going to wind up tonight, I'd purely like to get winding."

"Missus Semple," Ben said admiringly, "you got to be part Injun. Your tongue don't wobble one damned bit."

"Name's Ellie, cowboy—to you."

Ben felt a trifle warm. He shifted to a safer place. "Ruel," he ordered, "push on. We're primed."

"Yes sir. Miz Semple, you kindly crawl in the middle twixt me and Mr. Ben. There's some scary spots along the way up. Watch her, Mr. Ben."

The inside trail proved all that had been hinted.

In place after place it dropped straight off into hellish pits where the candle's gleam vanished into the deeps of emptiness. Far below they could hear the splashing of dislodged rocks into some water many times the depth of Little Big Canyon Creek. Rats, the seeming size of small pigs, scurried and chittered in the dark. Again, entire vaults erupted in noisome clouds of disturbed hibernating bats, their fetid bodies and foul odors now bumping, now choking the human crawlers along the ledge. It was an interminable journey creeping upward on raw hands and barked knees. By its ending Elvira Semple was a wrack of dry sobs, utterly exhausted in nerve and mind. Ben ached to throttle Ruel Oakes. Yet when, finally, they topped out in the main heading of the Old Glory, the tall man understood for the first time what chance the drifter youth had seen in coming back to Canyon Creek—felt for the first time his own excitement rise.

The ghost-guarded diggings were a supernatural fortress. Any half-professional, ex-Confederate outlaw with two years' experience along the frontier owlhoot trail would have to recognize the hideout of all hideouts when he saw it. Old Pegleg's Montana mine was the winner, hands down. It made Utah's Robbers' Roost, Wyoming's Hole-in-the-Wall, and Missouri's Little Blue limestone caves all look like prairie-dog kennels. Why, great God Amighty, from a place like this it might actually be possible to guerrilla-raid the vigilantes. Maybe even to get it out of them why, first Ben Allison, then Ruel Oakes, had been tarred with murders they did not commit. Especially it might, for the

81

stranglers believed both of their framed-up victims to be already dead.

Who would know Ben and the boy were there?

Who would even imagine it?

Jesus! It was a real gunfighter's chance.

There remained, of course, the matter of the Semple woman, but Ben was working on that. Next morning they would get up before first light, then they would catch old Poo Cat, saddle him up, put the woman on his back, and send the both of them off on the high lope for Shafter's Store. Hell, the gelding could have them there in an hour or so the way he traveled. And the Shafters were good people. They would take the woman in and help her on her way to Wyoming; that was settled in Ben's mind.

"Folks," he said to his companions, "she is deep enough for today. What do you say we turn in?"

Neither Ruel Oakes nor Elvira Semple argued it.

Shortly, only the sounds of bone-deep slumber echoed in the mountain hall of Walter "Pegleg" Gates.

19

The vigilantes met in the rear tackroom of the Blue Light Livery Barn shortly before 11:00 P.M. the night of the posse's return from the abortive chase after Ruel Oakes and the Texas outlaw, Ben Allison. The attendees, board members only, were tense with the fatigues and doubts of the manhunt compounded by Draco's unexpected blue-ticketing of the popular Elvira Semple. Sensing their mood, the Executive proceeded cautiously.

"The case of the Semple woman," he began, "must be considered on its merits, not its emotions. That is why I have called you here—that and the unfortunate course of our pursuit of the Negro rapist and murderer. These affairs pose a definite threat to the public support for our committee here in Canyon Creek. Steps must be taken at once to bolster the discipline of this chapter."

He eyed the silent board members: Executive Assistant Jack Spain; Sergeant-at-Arms Wayce L. "Fat" Fleeger; Company Scout Napoleon "Frenchy" Burloign; new Recording Secretary George Lambert; charter members Selkirk Johnson, Doud Harriman, Dansk Jensen, W. T. Harris.

"As for the community," he continued watchfully, "it must be brought to understand, finally, that the high duty of this Vigilance Committee of Canyon Creek, Montana Territory, is to provide swift and humane justice where the law fails to do so.

"The committee must never be permitted to forget the same sacred assignment." He swept them with his good eye narrowed. "Last midnight, and today on the trail, an air of rebellion—of defection if you will—was manifestly evident. This chapter wavers. It must be held."

Once again the mismated eyes challenged his listeners.

"The chair accepts suggestions," he said grimly.

It seemed no one would answer and the Executive was on the point of reading them the act of his own scriptures for holding together the Canyon Creek Committee, when Dansk Jensen arose and said quietly, "Mr. Draco, I quit."

"Fat!" rasped Selman Draco. "Bar the door!"

The blacksmith flexed thick shoulders. "Somebody will be hurt," he said softly to Fleeger. "Please let me pass."

"Fat," Draco gritted, "arrest him."

Doud Harriman, editor of the camp newspaper, found his feet. "For God's sake, what have we come to here?" he demanded. "Let the man go!"

"Doud," said Jack Spain, drawing his gun and joining Fleeger at the door, "back off. You were an oath-founder of this chapter. You know no one quits the committee."

"By God!" Harriman cried. "That's not good enough for me any more." He wheeled on the others. "How about it, boys? She deep enough for anybody else?"

Selman Draco's bad eye bulged. Invisibly swift, he drew a Colt's Navy Caliber .36-percussion revolver.

"No one will leave," he said.

The impasse was dissolved by Dansk Jensen. Noting the rapt attention of all to the conflict between Draco and the editor, the immensely strong blacksmith stepped in behind Spain and Fleeger, seized them up by their necks, and cracked their skulls ringingly together. Fleeger weighed in excess of two hundred fifty pounds; Spain was not a small man. Their combined crash to the planked floor bounced haybales and rattled coal-oil lanterns on their hooks.

"Ya," announced Dansk calmly, straightening from his inspection of the numbed bodies, "we go, friend Harriman."

They went out into the barn proper, closing the door behind them. There was no pursuit. Draco holstered his weapon. "Let the record show they violated Rule Nine," he said to George Lambert. "This meeting is adjourned."

"Not quite," denied Frenchy Burloign. "We want to know about Elvira Semple. We know Rule Nine, but what about the woman? We all liked her. Why did you not?"

"I read the charge in the street," said Draco carefully. "You heard it. Four decent women of this camp testified their men received favors of this woman without fee proper, and not in the Oriental or its adjacent wagons. Read Rule Five. This sort of thing does not go in any mining camp of the Rocky Mountains. Do you doubt the four women?"

"Never, *patron,* I doubt their husbands."

"You expect the husbands to confront the town?"

"If they don't, *patron,* it's hearsay testimony."

"Don't lecture me on the law, Burloign!"

Selkirk Johnson, a notably butt-headed man, stood forth.

"Frenchy's square-on as a packmule's ass, Draco. You can't wedge your way past what he says."

Draco went livid. "The woman was *convicted*," he said.

"*Oui,* that may be the trouble, *patron.*" Napoleon Burloign held the trail. "Too much convicting. First the mulatto boy, then the Texas drifter, finally our poor small *fille de joie*. No real evidence, *patron*. Just convictions."

The disfigured eye bulged anew. "Are you charging a connection of these things, Burloign? Against me?"

The Canuck breed turned away without answer. "You will need a new company scout," he said. "She is deep enough for me, *mes amis*." He went out past Fleeger and Spain, who were just recovering their senses at the exit.

"Well," Draco said to Selkirk Johnson, his rage strangely quieted, "will you also go, or close the door and stay?"

"I signed the charter," nodded the stubborn one, and reshut the outer door. "Meeting still adjourned?"

Selman Draco seemed satisfied. "It is," he said. Then, to Lambert: "Blow out the lights, George. Look for a clear way before stepping into the street. There will be a full meeting tomorrow for Rule Nine warrants."

He meant certificates of execution, the dreaded "blue tickets" of the vigilantes. The men all hung heads, nodding their understanding of the necessity yet feeling its deadliness in their very guts. Lambert shaded the chimneys and puffed out the lampwicks. The darkness was instant, acrid with coal-oil smoke, inky-black. The men felt their ways toward the tackroom door.

They had not reached it when someone outside was pounding upon it demandingly.

85

20

"Who's there?" Draco said, ear to door.

"It's me, Ratsmith," a reedy voice answered. "I got something for you."

"All right, what is it? Say it and be gone."

"Can't say it, got to show it to you. You interested?"

The men waited on their leader's reply. They all knew Fagan Ratsmith, the twisted little man with the hunched back and withered, dragging leg. He was one of those toadying vermin familiar to every frontier community. He saw, heard, or in some way found out about everything that went forward by day or night in Canyon Creek, and held it all for sale at the highest bid.

"Well?" Jack Spain challenged Draco.

"I'll talk to him," the Executive decided. "You men go on out the back way by the root cellar. Go quietly. No use having Ratsmith spread it around that he hit a board meeting. Quickly, now. All of you."

Fleeger, Spain, and Harris at once entered the trap door which led into the dug cellar behind the barn and the vigilantes' emergency-exit route. Selkirk Johnson neither moved to depart nor to be quiet. "I'm a'going with you," he informed Draco. "Time somebody was tailing you."

Instantly, he felt Draco's Navy Colt in his side.

"Go with the others!" the Executive whispered. "Now."

The obstinate Johnson replied to the order with a bony elbow brought up hard into the side of Draco's head. The leader staggered back, but the Colt did not discharge. Selkirk kicked open the door disdainfully. The blow surprised the eavesdropping Ratsmith, knocking him backward over a large metal-lidded oat bin. Johnson, unaware of the accident, strode on past the bin, determined to join editor Harriman and blacksmith Jensen in alerting the camp to the disintegration of Selman Draco's stewardship of the Canyon Creek Vigilance Committee. He was some ten steps upon his way when struck from behind by a manure shovel which was in the hands of the Executive. Moaning in vital hurt, he went down and lay still.

Draco dragged him by the feet to the oat bin and stuffed him into it. He then drew the Navy Colt, slid it in under the reclosed lid, and fired three muffled shots point-blank into the head of Selkirk Johnson. Straightening, the Executive's glance swept the interior of the old barn.

Up by the street doors, closed now against the winter night, he saw the feeble throw of the liveryman's lantern wicked to lowest setting. In the boarded stall beyond the lantern, where Juke Coleridge lived his life of quiet misery as chief swamper of the Blue Light, all was dark silence save for the providential snoring of Coleridge which, in the barn's echoing stillness, thundered like the clap of doom made into joyous testament of "no witnesses" for Selman Draco's brutal killing of the hapless Johnson.

All right.

There remained only the problem of the camp's clear discontent with the leadership of Selman Draco stemming from the uncalled-for deaths of good citizens Thomas Clarke, Edward Dobbs, August Wendler, and Charles Farwood in the badly managed manhunt which had split the posse at gallows tree flat to begin the simmering revolt.

Well, it was a dangerous prospect, no question of it.

But Draco forced his toiling mind to function in its deadly pattern. There had to be a way out; a man need only remember that God had not made him as ordinary men are made. His enemies in Canyon Creek were

87

common men with common minds and common gifts. They must never be permitted to defy nor bring to trial Selman Draco, destroying his great dream. He had found his ultimate place in Montana Territory and built his base of power in the vigilante movement precisely as Nathan Stark before him. Now, at the very threshold of success, fate was seeking to deny Selman Draco.

Why else had the mulatto boy Ruel Oakes chosen this remote place of Canyon Creek, in all the Rocky Mountains, to appear like a specter out of the curse of a man's past to haunt him in the very hour of victory?

What but the very will of hell could have brought the cringing devil to thus seek out the master he once had known two thousand miles and a thousand days away?

And then, when Selman Draco would destroy the speckled albatross, sealing his black lips forever, why had all those damnable Canyon Creekers met their deaths in the cause? Those deaths which now had good committeemen down in the drinking places and harlotries of the camp, multiplying their vicious canards against their faithful Executive and the movement he championed. What one thing in an unfair God's name had started all of this?

Selman Draco knew the answer.

The Texas cowboy-outlaw.

It had all turned wrong at the point where tall Ben Allison had ridden into the vigilantes' midst at gallows tree flat, with a vigilante price on his own head, to save the life of young Ruel Oakes.

But Ruel Oakes was dead and Ben Allison was dead.

Shades of the departed did not testify against the living. Ghosts were not his enemies and Selman Draco did not fear the quick above the ground. Selkirk Johnson had learned that too late, so had all the others back through the violent years. Now it must be the same for those remaining—yet who truly remained?

Could the thick-headed Jensen harm him? The

weakling Harriman? The Cree-breed Burloign? What did they know that might bring hurt to Selman Draco? Nothing.

Vigilante justice did not need a living eyewitness, but the constituted law of the territory did. So the stranglers would never try Executive Draco. He would demand a miners' court and open justice if ever caught and accused, but who was left to accuse him?

Only someone who could say he had seen Selman Draco strike the fatal blow.

And there was no such one.

The chills and the sweating subsided. The gaunt body, tensed near the oat bin, eased visibly. The darkness hid all. Tomorrow's sun would reveal nothing. Selkirk's body would be long since removed to some safer crypt and no man would remain alive to say that Selman Draco had brought it there. He would require a horse, that was all. A sure-footed single beast to bear away the noisome burden. And he had an entire barnful from which to choose.

"Yes, a horse," he muttered aloud. "A good horse."

As the words broke he heard a scurrying as of departing vermin in distant rafters. But it was only the misshapen cripple Fagan Ratsmith who limped into view from the musty gloom, knuckling his brow and simpering.

"A horse you say, Mr. Draco? Aha, and what is it you think old Ratsmith has brung you, hee hee hee! Come along and see, right here in this very stall, hee hee."

Something deep within Draco, a force of evil as black as the pit of his hatreds, forewarned the leader of the stranglers that Ratsmith had brought him a horse of horses, a gift of certain death—for the enemies of Selman Draco—and so he stayed the Navy Colt and followed the informer to the stall.

He heard the cripple saying, "Easy, easy," to the animal. Then he himself was up with Ratsmith, peering through the darkness at *what* horse the hunchback had thought worth bringing to the Canyon Creek Committee of the Vigilantes of Montana.

It was the horse that it must be.

It was the Comanche mustang pony of the dead Texas cowboy Ben Allison.

21

Fleeger and Jack Spain said good-night to W. T. Harris in the alleyway behind the Blue Light. When the new recording secretary had disappeared, the two men spoke in quick, guarded tones, then split up, one going around the livery barn on each side toward Main Street. Reaching the front of the structure, they saw nothing but the empty, frozen mud of the street. Draco and the hunchback were still inside. The henchmen waited.

In a short time the street doors creaked and Draco and Ratsmith came out, Draco leading a horse bearing a sacked body. Neither of the Executive's men recognized the pony until it passed Fleeger's end of the barn, going south on Main. Fleeger at once stepped out of hiding.

"Hold it, Mr. Draco," he said. He patted the corpse fraternally. "Anybody we know?"

Behind them, the crunch of Jack Spain's boots in the icy mud warned Draco to go warily. "What the devil do you mean trailing me? You had your orders." He spoke low-voiced and Jack Spain, coming up, took his cue from that. "Yes sir," he answered softly for Fleeger, "but we just got to worrying about the membership being so edgy."

Both men dropped hands to revolver butts and

Draco understood that they were demanding to be let in on whatever it was he and Ratsmith might be about.

"I was going to send for you," he said, "but Ratsmith wanted to show me something first."

"Like what?" asked Fat Fleeger.

"Yeah," said Spain, "a nice plot for old Selkirk?"

Draco frowned, scanning the deserted street. The Oriental and the other places would begin emptying before long now. Any moment could bring a curious Canyon Creeker to join the onlookers of the Comanche mustang captured by Fagan Ratsmith. Or several of same. And God knew what the feelings of the town might presently be with editor Harriman buying the drinks and using a newspaperman's dirty ways to burgeon the filth against the local committee and its Executive. Seemingly, or at least hopefully, he had not yet succeeded in getting anything lethal whipped up. But time was shrinking in the late-night cold.

"Come on, then," he said to his henchmen. "We can't stand here. Let the horse out, Ratsmith. Hurry."

The informer let go the gelding's headstall and kept hold of the lead rope. "Go on, horse," he said. "Hee-yah!"

Given its head, the mustang went briskly out along the road south to the Bozeman turnoff. Here, the pony swung east along the Bozeman branch for a half mile, then left the wagon ruts to cut into the open snow for the timber behind Ghost Hill. The men following panted and cursed to keep pace, but they now knew something strange, perhaps foreboding, lay in the Indian pony's actions. It required no urging from Draco to spur Fleeger and Spain. The only thing, indeed, that slowed the group was the dragging leg of Fagan Ratsmith. And after they left the Bozeman Road, Draco lifted the crippled informer onto the mustang's back, taking the lead rope himself. In this swifter way, they came within the hour to the place where Little Big Canyon Creek disappeared into the mountain of old Pegleg Gates. Five minutes after that, Ratsmith had found them the snow-printed tracklines of three humans going across

91

Little Big Canyon, and then ordered the Comanche mustang freed to "show them what Fagan Ratsmith had to sell the Canyon Creek Committee."

Draco unloaded Johnson's body and turned the pony loose.

Whinnying happily, the mustang took to the tracklines like a trailing bluetick hound, running the telltale footsteps squarely to the black cavern where the stream rushed into Ghost Hill. There it stopped and made mustang sounds, nosed the snow, stamped several times as if puzzled, then wandered off to browse willowbark along the creek. Ratsmith caught him up by the dragging lead-rope, then returned to Selman Draco and his two henchmen.

"I seen them prints by lantern," he told Draco. "Got my old bull's-eye lamp from my shack yonder." He pointed around the curve of Ghost Hill, where he had a rickety cabin built into the ridgeside above the timber. "Spotted them real good. One's a big feller wearing Texas boots; one's a not-so-big feller with brokedown brogans; other's a woman."

"A woman?"

"As ever was—with dancehall shoes, pointy toes, and all. Makes a track no bigger'n a minute with thirty seconds sawed off."

"Ellie Semple," said Jack Spain, eying the others.

"Got to be," agreed Fat Fleeger.

Draco shook his head. The skull-like face was gray with cold and fatigue. "It's crazy," he muttered, "crazy."

Fagan Ratsmith laughed.

"Ghosts," he chortled squeakily. "Ghosts in old Ghost Ridge. Hee hee hee!"

"It ain't crazy," Jack Spain answered Draco. "It's them. Ghosts don't make no Texas boot tracks."

"Yeah," said Fat Fleeger, "they don't unsaddle no Comanche geldings and turn them loose, neither." He paused. "They're in the mountain, Mr. Draco. With that damned whore that knows about Billie Dove— what we going to do?"

The Canyon Creek Executive turned to the snigger-

92

ing cripple who had led them there, voice deadly flat.

"Ratsmith," he said, "answer the man's question."

"Hee hee," chuckled the hunchback, "hee hee hee!"

"He's daft as a bat," Fat Fleeger said. "Forget him. He just got a rope and halter on that damn Injun pony, figured out these-here tracks to be them of the Texican cowboy and the nigger kid come back from where we thought they was dead, and reckoned we'd pay handsome to know that much."

"Yeah," Spain nodded, "you know Ratsmith. He's in every saloon and back alley in the camp. He's heard the bad-mouthing of us. What the hell? Half the posse come back here yesterday with their craws full of—" he paused awkwardly, then plunged on—"well, hell, Draco, of you and the way you went after the mulatto kid. We don't need to wait for Jensen, Frenchy, and Harriman to get started. This committee's in trouble, Draco, meaning you. Me and Fat heard it all over camp before you called the board meeting at the Blue Light tonight."

"They don't understand!" raged Draco suddenly. "Goddamn them all! They don't know I want the power to make this territory a better place for *them*, not for Selman Draco! The committee must stand. If it falls, I fall; the law will fall with me and the territory with the law. These ghosts have got to be laid! These murderers of the poor Vardeen creature must be—"

"Draco," Spain said sharply. "Make sense. You're rambling. Me and Fat are in this with you up to our goddamn gullets. The hell with the territory. It's *us* you're talking about. Don't give us any of that 'poor Vardeen creature' bull, you hear me? It's me, Jack Spain. That's Wayce Fleeger with me. We *knew about* you and Billie Dove."

"Christ Jesus, Mr. Draco!" shrilled Fat Fleeger. "Jack's right. After tonight this camp's going to be too shrunk to chamber any of the three of us. These-here 'ghosts' ashowing up make it the last stick of chaff out of the straw baler."

The Executive was as quickly subdued as he had

been raised to fury. The pains within his misshapen skull were crucifying him with their agony, but the singular force of the damaged brain thrust itself beyond the suffering. He nodded, wiping the water from his bad eye, his voice in its old dry-rattler buzz of controlled menace.

"All we need do is find Allison and the nigger boy, before they get to the Alder Gulch Committee and to that filthy Jewish lawyer of Nathan Stark's at Virginia City."

"My God!" Spain said. "I'd forgot that; it's why they come back!"

"Got to be," Fat Fleeger wheezed. "That cowboy told us that, remember? He wanted the Jew brung out for him to surrender the boy and him to. Son of a bitch!"

"Fat," Jack Spain muttered. "You smelling what I'm smelling in this-here ghost hunt?"

"I'm smelling something. What's tickling your nose?"

"Suppose we don't find the nigger kid and the cowboy? Suppose they get on up to Virginia and turn themselves in to the Jew? You know what's going to happen? Canyon Creek's going to install a miners' court that will hear out the Billie Dove murder down to the last witness in Montana Territory. And you know where that's going to wind up me and you at?"

"Where?" gulped Fat Fleeger.

"With *him*," Spain said, jerking a thumb at Draco. *"On the same limb."*

"Hee hee hee!" gurgled Fagan Ratsmith. "Two more for the sycamore." Then, querulously, "Where at's my money?"

"Oh, Christ Jesus," whimpered Fleeger, "we didn't kill nobody. How can they strangle us, Jack?"

"We know who did. It's the same thing," Spain said.

"I want my pay—two ghosts and a live female woman." The hunchback scuttled up to Draco. "I'm a'going up to the Gulch tomorry, Mr. Draco. Business

94

there. Seems like lawyer Lazarus pays good for ghosts."

Draco struck for him, pinned him by the throat. The rattler-button voice burred its deadly warning. "Ratsmith, one more word and you're dead. You will get your money when your work is done."

When he wheeled back upon Fleeger and Spain, he found himself covered by two drawn revolvers.

"Fat," Spain ordered, "get the horse from Ratsmith."

Fleeger did so, leading the mustang back to where his fellow henchman covered Draco. "There ain't no other way, Mr. Draco," the fat committeeman apologized. "She is way too deep for me and Jack, and we are going for Wyoming while there's yet dark to do it by."

Jack Spain and the fat vigilante mounted double on the nervous Indian pony, revolvers still playing on Selman Draco. "We've wrote too many blue tickets not to savvy when we're due to get billed ourselves," Spain told the silent Executive. "Them damn magpies the Virginia Committee warned Ben Allison about ain't been fed yet. Breakfast comes early, Draco. Watch your good eyeball."

The Executive raised a hand, delaying them. In reasoned tones he told the two that all might yet be won, if they would but hold fast to his cause. However, he understood their fears and could not blame them. If, after hearing his plea, they now would continue their ways, then all that Selman Draco could do was wish them godspeed. They had been good and faithful soldiers in the cause of the law in that cruel land. He would see that a just history remembered them for that. He held no ill against them, but wished mightily that they would stay.

"What do you say, men?" he concluded earnestly. "Will you help me?"

Jack Spain shook his head.

"You are past help, Draco," he said, and put heels to the Texas mustang.

Without anger Selman Draco drew the Navy Colt, leveled its octagon barrel to a steady sighting between

95

the shoulderblades of Fleeger. The fat rider gasped and fell sideways off the loping pony. Spain, turning to see what had happened, received the second bullet full in the face. He spun off the back of the mustang, the wiry animal crouching and leaping away in full gallop.

The snow gathered atop Jack Spain. He did not move within its cold embrace. But his comrade, Fleeger, not yet dead, strained to his knees in the drift where he had fallen and Selman Draco, walking over unhurriedly, put the barrel of the Colt into the fat man's sagging mouth and blew out the rear of his skullpan.

Wiping off the weapon, the Executive went back to where Fagan Ratsmith waited by the dark cavern of Little Big Canyon Creek's entrance into the mountain.

"Ratsmith," he said, placing the gun's muzzle carefully between the cripple's eyes, "you will take me to where they have gone or, by God, your brains will splatter the snow four rods around."

22

Ben came awake.

The stillness in the old mine pressed upon the ears. The stub of miner's candle carried by Ruel Oakes had gone out, drowned in its residual pool of tallow. Ben listened for the breathing of his companions, then sat bolt-upright when he heard only the restive sighing of Ellie Semple. He did not have to feel for the mulatto boy's weary form between himself and the camp woman. Ruel was gone.

"Missus," Ben said, "wake up."

"I'm awake, cowboy. Who could sleep with the way you snore and your colored friend sleepwalks?"

"You knowed he was gone?"

"He left the minute he thought we were both asleep. But in my work we don't drop off that good nor often. It doesn't pay."

"I wish," the big Texan said, "you wouldn't talk that way, ma'am."

"Oh?" Ellie Semple sat up, stretching. "Why?"

"It don't count with me."

"The hell you say." The woman's words were more bittersweet than mean. "You know what I am, Tex. It counts."

Ben found the melted-down candle in the dark. Digging out its mired wick, he relit it. The feeble tongue of brief light wavered. "It ain't no crystal chandellyer," he said, "but this place gives me the medium creeps."

"Me, too, cowboy. Thanks."

"Well, it won't last more'n long as a lynx-tail, but you're welcome no matter, ma'am."

"I don't mean the damn candle. Why don't you just shut up?"

It seemed to Ben that for some strange reason the aging dancehall girl was getting ready to weep again, and that wasn't fair of her. She just wasn't the crying kind.

"I reckon I can't, missus," he told her regretfully. "Something's wrong here. I can taste it; it's that rank."

Ellie Semple gave up the idea of sleep. Straightening her hair, she looked at Ben Allison. "You're so dumb," she said. "I guess that's what does it."

"Does what, ma'am?"

"Gives you your fatal appeal, cowboy." She intensified her look and, in the candlelight, Ben could see that her eyes were a wild smoky green in color and slanted just that come-hither way that made a special woman so female. There was enough of the light left over to show him something else too; Mrs. Elvira Semple did have that certain red hair he had known she must and also that cast of Latin good looks to her face

97

which again, as he had correctly guessed, guaranteed some mix of south-of-the-border blood in the Canyon Creek adventuress. It shook a man to have that kind of a woman giving him that kind of a look, and Ben showed it. His companion laughed, showing a dazzle of white teeth. "It's all right," she smiled, "I never charge a friend."

Ben got red, had trouble with his breathing.

"I ain't said you was a lady," he finally managed angrily, "but I don't care to drive the herd back and forwards over the other thing, either, you hear? I like you."

It was a blush, no question of it. It surprised Ellie Semple as much as it did the tall cowboy. "I will be damned," she said. "You colored me."

Ben put his head down, said nothing.

After a minute, he questioned the woman as to how long Ruel Oakes had been gone. She said at least six hours, maybe a lot more. It depended on how much she herself had dozed. Ben allowed this was scant help and they had best be up and doing, since he had reason to suspect from past experience the quality of the mulatto youth's dependability or, at very kindest, his good judgment. "It ain't that I don't trust him," he explained, "providing he ain't out of sight."

"Well," shrugged Ellie Semple, "he's your nig——" She broke off, finished awkwardly, "He's your colored man or kid, whichever. Anyway, you know him; I don't."

Ben nodded, a frown creasing his dark forehead.

"Happen you didn't know him," he asked, "how come you bore such hard witness against him?"

"I didn't."

"He says different, says it was your word turned the vigilantes against him—yours and Draco's."

"I only said what I knew, and that was him talking to me about Billie Dove last thing before they found her with his ax sunk into her head." She shook as to a chill, then controlled herself. "Mister, if you don't think a pretty-slim girl, only nineteen years old, with a nig— with a damn drifter's camp-ax struck to the haft in her

98

full face is something terrible to stumble onto, you better think again. It made me vomit, and nearly does now, just remembering."

"Anybody could have used his ax, missus. How come you didn't think of that? He says it was stole from him."

"You crazy, cowboy? Who was going to believe him against Selman Draco?"

"What do you mean? How come it was him and Draco?"

"Draco knew it was his ax; he'd seen it up to his camp on Ghost Ridge. You know, this old mine, here."

"How come you to find your friend?"

"We lived together in that old trapper's shack up the back alley from the livery barn. You know the one?"

"Yep."

"Well, when Draco came into the Oriental early and asked where Billie was, I told him she must be at the shack as she was late by an hour already for work that night. We're supposed to be on the job at least an hour before the main trade sets in. It gets things started."

"I reckon," Ben said. "So then what?"

"I asked Draco to go and get her, but he said he had to meet a man and why didn't I go fetch her? Naturally, somebody had to. We got docked if we were half an hour late. So I went over to the shack."

"And there she was, Ruel's ax and all."

"Yes."

"How come you figure Draco didn't want to go and get her, ma'am? I mean, you was busy on your job."

"Don't be simple-minded, cowboy. Mr. Selman Draco was your Canyon Creek Vigilante Executive man. He was second only to Nathan Stark in the stranglers in the whole territory. You think such a pillar of the decent folk is going to be fetching a whore out of her house right in front of God and the good wives of Canyon Creek, Montana?"

"Not the way you put it," Ben nodded. "Say, missus, why was your friend late for work anyhow? She sick?"

"Sick to puking. She was going to have a kid, about three months along. Nobody knew it."

"Nobody, ma'am?"

"Not unless it was Draco."

"Him again? How come him?"

"Because Billie said so."

"She said he was the daddy, you mean?"

"She didn't just say so; he was."

"And you never peeped about that at the vigilante hearing?"

"Would you, mister?"

"I dunno rightly."

"Well, you think about it. Didn't they blue-ticket you right square after a U.S. judge turned you loose up to Bozeman? That's the story we got from up to Virginia."

"Yeah, they did."

"What you think they would have done to me had I testified against their Executive? Or worse yet just spread it around camp on my own?"

Ben nodded, knowing what the stranglers would have done. "That's why Draco stirred up the town to run you out, eh? You was purely lucky he didn't do more."

"Well, hell, even the stranglers aren't hanging women yet. So that's no credit to him."

"Didn't mean it was," Ben Allison answered softly.

"Well what more is it you do mean?"

"What he done to your friend."

"You're demented. Billie? Draco killed Billie?"

"Sure as hell don't frost over, ma'am. He done it."

"Oh, my God." The green eyes shimmered with the near-tears of overwrought memories. "What will we do? What *can* we do?"

"Come on," Ben said, standing up and blowing out the candlewick in its vanished pool of tallow, "we can get you up to Virginia City, that's what. You tell that story to Esau Lazarus and you will see a brand of law burned onto this camp in open miners' court that will set the stranglers back to taw and elevate Selman

Draco higher than he ever dreamed to go among the Vigilantes of Montana."

"Lazarus? You mean Nathan Stark's lawyer?"

"I know them both. Stark don't unbutton his pants without old Esau signals him it's time. How come you think Stark come so far so fast? It's the old Jew, believe it. He's smart as a three-legged weasel, square as a plum-bobbed barn. He's the *real* law, Missus Semple; we get to him, we win. But first we got to get there."

Ellie Semple had heard the truth. She believed it and was ready. "All right, cowboy; let's get there," she said. "Where do we start?"

"With two good horses," Ben replied.

"Oh, Christ," said the woman feelingly, but the big Texan only grinned. "We will rent them," he said. "I am opposed to thieving and there is no time to climb around the outside of this mountain alooking for Poo Cat on the far side."

"Rent horses? In the middle of the night? Us?"

"Why, surely, yes indeed," said Ben. "From the Blue Light Livery Barn. I will have Mr. Coleridge to put it on my bill."

"You *are* ill in the head!" cried Ellie Semple. "I won't go with you!"

"You rather wait for Draco?"

"You damn bastard!"

"Whatever's fair," Ben said.

He started for the mine exit and Ellie Semple delayed at least a full two seconds before lifting her skirts, taking a hard tuck in her old cloth coat, and racing over the rubble of the tunnel floor to follow him.

Yet neither reached the ore-dump outside.

From behind them came the shadowed lancings of a mine candle, approaching the drift from a stope tunnel slanted sharply down into the mountain. With the candlelight came hoarse panting and a sliding sound of scrambling feet in loose rock. Next instant a ragged, long-haired figure stumbled up out of the stope tunnel,

101

gasping for them to wait. It was Ruel Oakes, and with news of the night which put the Blue Light Livery Barn as far away as the winter moon: Selman Draco was in the mountain, his guide the crippled ghost of Walter "Pegleg" Gates.

23

Ruel's story held Ben and Ellie Semple enthralled.

It could not have been, yet they knew it *was*.

When he had come to Canyon Creek, the boy said, hunger and ill treatment in the camp had driven him to the high refuge of the Old Glory Mine. His southern plantation experience before freedom had taught him much of the lore of haunts and specters and so, when he heard of an old abandoned shafthead which was the shunned by the Canyon Creekers, he retreated there. His reasoning was that haunts were more easily lived with than live white people. He held no great affection for ghosts, then or now, but all the same he was starving down in the town and freezing from exposure to the cruel Montana winter. To a gaunt mulatto wanderer the old mine promised warmth and hiding and, most of all, security from intrusion or punishment by the campfolk below.

It had been a hard life. But using the skills of his Mississippi boyhood, he fashioned wire snares and traps from the debris of the mine's dump and, with old camp-ax and pocketknife, he managed to stave off disaster. Within ten days he had made a home for himself in the same antechamber to the main drift in which they now crouched. The old mine furnished everything from firewood to steel for striking a fire, fresh water, candles, headlamps for exploration, timbers for stretching his rabbit hides—all that a plantation-born boy had to have to fend for himself.

The haunts had not bothered him until the third day of his residence, then the strange cries and echoing moans commenced back in the far reaches of the tunnelings. It was a frightening thing, but the mining camp below was more so. Making up certain wooden figurines to ward off evil, taught him by his African-born mother, Ruel had taken six candles, a rabbit-fur sling full of smoked meat, a headlamp, and his trusty knife and set out into the mountain to meet the ghost who lived there. He did not take his ax because he knew such weapons to be useless against the other world. The knife, of course, was only habit. A boy never left his knife behind; it went with his pants.

After crawling and falling through tunnels and side drifts and down into stopes, he began to see the uselessness of his mission. The ghost cries which at first lured him along were now silent and, after hours of hard work at following the mazelike turns of old Pegleg's incredible warren, Ruel decided to go back.

It was not to be thought, he assured his rapt listeners at this point, that he had just taken off into the tangle of tunnels without a method and a plan. Down home at Drakehurst, the six-thousand-acre plantation of his white family, near Chupelo, Mississippi, there had been a great system of caves in the ancient stone ledges above the river. Ruel had learned the strange wisdoms and instincts of the spelunkers—the cave people—in those vast river caverns, as all young slaves were taught them, against that day when life itself might be the forfeit of *not* knowing where to go in the sightless earth. Hence, when he went after the siren calls of the old prospector's noisy shade, he had done so with consummate care and skill to memorize in reverse, like reading letters backward in a mirror, every thrust and double-back of the way. Here and there marking piles of stone chips were carefully erected, arrows drawn in the centuries-old dust of the rock floor and, in three key intersections of multiple tunnels, candles had been lit and left for beacons. But all of that came suddenly to naught.

The first warning when he turned back was that the last-placed beacon candle was blown out even as he crawled toward it from a distance. Even then he believed it to have been a mine draft and kept crawling. Yet when he had reached where it was, it was not where it had been, but in that empty place were hot tallow drippings and the acrid smoke of the damped wick. Ruel Oakes knew the candle had been *taken* and he knew that whatever it was in the mine with him was *not* a haunt or a phantom or a specter. A human being was in that mine, another one than himself, and it did not want Ruel Oakes to get back out of that mine. It had lured him into its very bowels and now was destroying his trailmarkers before he might come to them and what this meant was utter and terrible blackness in heart and mind, as well as blinking, fearful eye.

The ghost had led him to his death.

But why?

What possible harm could a miserable, driven-out, shivering colored boy from the Deep South do to that old mine or its ghost?

Suddenly, cringing there in the smoky darkness of that deep tunnel, he had known the answer.

The ghost *and* the old mine were hiding something.

A dark secret which no intruding searcher would find or share or spread the word of to others.

On his way from Mississippi to Montana, Ruel Oakes had been in a score of mining camps. The lure was always gold and the ultimate strike was the mother lode, the bonanza, the "place where it all came from."

So now he knew. Old Pegleg Gates had hit the main vein. He had found it all. Somewhere in that great mountain lay the treasurehouse of the Canyon Creek, perhaps of all the Virginia strikes, from Alder Gulch to Ghost Ridge.

"It were purely scary," said Ruel, interrupting himself. "Yonder I were, lost in the hind gut of the moun-

104

tain and thinking about onliest one thing—all that gold!"

"It just proves you're human," Ben said, "just like the rest of us."

"Go on," urged Ellie Semple. "How'd you get out?"

The mulatto youth made it short then. He had started on, his last candle in his headlamp. He had made a wrong turn, and knew it, when of a sudden his candle picked up a blaze of light like nothing he had ever seen or dreamed to see. Another scurry of crawling on and there, opening before him, was the bonanza—a stope big enough to hold the Blue Light Livery Barn without scraping the ridgepole—and from where Ruel Oakes lay on his belly in the tunnel's bore, he could see nothing along the walls, floor, and ore-vaulted ceiling but one unending blaze of the mother color.

"Then what for God's sake? What happened next?" It was Ben, breathing hard. He was seeing all that gold and feeling it. "Can you find it again? Christ Jesus, with that much bonanza ore we don't need Lazarus nor Nathan Stark nor nobody. God Amighty! Where is it?"

"Wait!" said Ellie Semple, the creature of a hard life herself and thinking now to preserve that life. "You said the ghost of Pegleg Gates was bringing Draco up here the way we came, through the bat cavern? That's crazy!"

"Not so," insisted Ruel Oakes, and told them why.

When he had found the bonanza, he had found the ghost of old Pegleg waiting there for him. Only it wasn't any ghost but the old man himself. He had been terribly injured in a roof-fall all those years before, but had lived and recovered unknown to any man. It was then he had invented his other life, so that he might go down into the camp for the things that he needed, both of the flesh and of the spirit. It pleasured him to devil the community which had laughed at him as a lunatic in life and so the revenging form of Fagan Ratsmith was born.

But the old fellow had proven unable, either as Walter Gates or Fagan Ratsmith, to murder the mulatto boy who now knew his vast secret of the golden stope. He had guided the boy back to the shafthead, sworn him to lifelong secrecy on a payment of one half the worth of the Old Glory should he be true to the trust, and so they had lived together in the Old Glory for many happy weeks until the fatal day when some-one had stolen Ruel's old camp-ax.

Ben and Mrs. Semple knew what came after that.

"Yes," Ben said urgently, "we know exactly what came after that, Ruel boy; it was Selman Draco that killed that poor Billie Dove of yours and Ellie and me figure to prove it on him. We got to get up to Virginia and fetch lawyer Lazarus for our case. We was just vamoosing when you showed."

"Well, we had better still vamoose!" said Ellie Semple. "I've got no mind to wait here for that crazy Draco. He will kill anything in his path. He's loon-mad, Ben."

She had never called him that and Ben noted it, while racing on in his mind to find their best move.

"It's not only him that's sick in his head," warned Ruel. "When Pegleg found out I'd brought you folks here, he figured I'd broke our promise. That's where I been these four hours gone—down the mountain auguring it with him. But he wouldn't hold with me. Said now everybody would have to stay in the mountain with him, and that was why he'd gone and fetched Mr. Draco. He's meaning to let him do his murdering for him, then just blow out the candles and leave him down in the gut of the ridge."

"Christ," said Ben, "it ain't sane, none of it."

"You're right it isn't," said Ellie Semple. "Come on, let's get shut of here for sure."

Ben was in agreement, but Ruel Oakes quickly pointed out that, if they fled outside upon the mountain, it would not resolve the matter of Selman Draco. The Vigilance Committee Executive could still gather posse enough of his stranglers to run them all down and finish for keeps what he had failed to do before. And he would not miss two times.

"You got a sticker there," Ben said. "We will just have to get him before he gets us. Right here."

"No, Mr. Ben. We still have to fetch the lawyer man. Remember? Me and you got our freedom to win yet. Don't do no human good to kill the man kilt Miss Billie. Gots to give him a trial, like you say in the beginning. Ain't no other way me and you going to be free."

Ben did not want to remember it, but he did.

Ruel Oakes was right.

He was only an ignorant cinnamon-colored speckled nigger kid but by God in heaven he was right.

"Pick up the pot, Ruel Oakes," he said. "We got to do both things at onct, however. You got to get Missus Semple here on up to Virginia. It's her story as will bring lawyer Lazarus to Canyon Creek, not yourn or mine. You understand that, boy?"

"He doesn't have to understand it!" snapped Ellie. "*I* understand it. What do you mean to do, meanwhile?"

Ben grinned the old pale-eyed wolf grin.

"Going to see how it feels to work the inside of the fence for a change," he said. "Going to arrest me a Canyon Creek strangler for murder and fetch him in to the Mason's Hall for fair trial."

He swung on Ruel Oakes.

"Boy," he charged him, "you get the lady up to Virginia and the old lawyer back down here to Canyon Creek. You'll find old Mr. Ben awaiting for you with Selman Draco at this end. That's a vow. Now take out!"

Again—and for the final time—Ruel balked.

No, he said. They would go as Mr. Ben directed but not the *way* he directed—not out the main drift hole of the Old Glory. They had to gain time, and also to get away for Virginia City unseen. There was but one way to do that and by the Lord's divine grace, Ruel Oakes knew that way.

"Come on, *please!*" he urged them. "Foller me."

Ben weighed it as Ellie Semple backed away from the mulatto youth, saying she wouldn't dream of following him back into that black mountain. But the big Texan knew the ragged drifter better than to place the dancehall woman's hesitations in the same scale with his, and he made his last choice without waiting.

He grabbed Ellie Semple by the arm, advised her to shut up "total," turned to the mulatto boy, and nodded low-voiced, "All right, Mr. Ruel Oakes. You're fol- lered."

At once, Ruel was off, leading them down into the mountain by a different, less difficult way than they had come up through it. Behind them, as they fled, Ben was shiveringly certain that he heard the ghostly cries of the guardian of Ghost Ridge, baying on their track like some spectral hound of hell. But when Ellie grew sorely afraid, he vowed stoutly that old mines echoed like that from wind drafts and up-sucks and shiftings of the mother rock, and for her to press on and stay close up with the mulatto boy.

She did so, cursing Ben.

After what seemed an eternity of stumbling, falling, head- and arm-scraping on the narrow tunnel sides and ceilings, Ruel called back that they were nearing the outside of the mountain. A minute later, without warn- ing, they emerged into the wildly impossible glow of the mother lode.

It was a stunning sight—a thing which literally stole the breath from the body. But the mulatto boy pushed onward through the gleaming vault, and, if they would not lose the light of his headlamp candle, they must go on with him. The blackness closing in so swiftly behind the disappearing youth was more powerful than the suddenly expunged glitter of the treasurehouse of Peg- leg Gates. Belatedly, they ran after him—Ellie sobbing, Ben Allison cursing.

When in this ragged fashion the three came truly to the outside of Ghost Ridge they did not break into the nature's cover of the mountainside, but rather, through a creaking, squealing door of rotting wood and iron- strap hinges, into the musty confines of a moldering, filthy prospector's shack: the timberline cabin of Fagan Ratsmith, hard around the fan of the great hill from the

108

entrance of Little Big Canyon Creek into the base rock, on the back side of Ghost Ridge and within easy mustang whistle of the faithfully waiting Comanche gelding, Puhakat, known as Poo Cat.

24

Draco and Ratsmith came panting to the drifthead antchamber so close behind the fugitives that the stink of Ruel's headlamp candle still lingered.

The Executive, exhausted by his passage of Bat Vault Cliff and Black Water Drop-off, fought to regain both breath and strength. The while, his sickened mind raced on.

No mining-country man could follow the crippled informer up through that mountain and escape the certainty that Fagan Ratsmith was more than he said he was. Instinctively, Draco understood the danger of this fact to his imperiled cause.

True, the rascal had lived for years in that verminous old shack halfway up the ridge, but that was on the back side of the mountain. Moreover, no witness in Canyon Creek had ever seen Ratsmith with pick, shovel, mine candle, headlamp, jackhammer, bullprod drill, blasting powder or any other tool of hardrock gold-digging description. Even so, he was not just a crazy old galoot living alone out in the lodgepole pine and aspen and willow brush of the high roughs along the Bozeman cutoff. No, Ratsmith might be old and crazy and a human packrat of a senile recluse but, by the gods of all gold strikes, he was no innocent when it came to mines and to minerals.

Who was Fagan Ratsmith then?

Draco reviewed the question now as he regained his

breath from the long crawl up through the mountain. The hunchback searched the anteroom of the drift and the outer flat of the ore-dump for sign of the three intruders who had come unbidden to see the very heart of his secret hill of gold. He had not reached any answer when Ratsmith returned from the dump.

"Gone," the old man sniffed. "Gone with the ghost, hee hee! Nary a sign yonder, nary a trace hither. Hee hee hee. I told you, Mr. Draco. The ghost got them."

The Executive seized him by the neck.

"You saw me shoot those two traitors down on the creek. I suspect you know what happened to Selkirk Johnson. Do you think it will be any different with you, you limping, misshapen old fool?"

"No, no, you wouldn't harm old Ratsmith!"

"Try me one more time," said Selman Draco. "I will give you a taste to help you decide." He choked the poor creature until his veins bulged and his eyeballs protruded, then slacked off and struck him on the back to get his breathing started up again. There was a retching near-vomitous moment when it seemed the informer would not rally. But he was as tough as he was strange and, after a bad bit of gasping, came around and could talk.

"All right," nodded Draco, releasing him. "You still say the ghost got them?"

"But I don't foller it, Mr. Draco. I swear to God I don't. That darkie boy, now, he must of knowed some other way to go. I vow you there ain't a footprint outside in that dump snow, and you can see for half a mile either way."

"You saying they have to be in the mountain?"

"As ever was. Less'n they can fly."

"Find them," Draco buzzed in his flat rattler voice.

Ratsmith started to delay again, then realized from the mad gleam in the other man's unmatched eyes that his own life would be forfeit without further warning if he stretched his companion's sanity another unknown mite. It was a case of the mad knowing the mad, and Fagan Ratsmith was Shakespearian in his own afflic-

110

tion—daft only when the wind lay in a certain direction. When it shifted, he knew a sluicebox from a blasting cap.

"Yes, yes," he hastened to reply. "Hee hee, friend Draco. Look here, over where my candle shines on the dust of this old down-chute here. You see what I see?"

The Executive stumbled to his side. Deeply printed in the rubble of the steep tunnel's down-pitching floor he saw the same tracklines as beyond Little Big Canyon Creek these several hours gone. If those prints in the outer snow had been those of big Ben Allison, the Semple woman, and the Negro boy, then down that dark and fearsome-narrow hole in the mother rock had gone, perhaps only minutes before himself and Fagan Ratsmith, the three people in all Montana Territory he must find and kill before daybreak.

"Ratsmith," he barked, gathering himself for the descent into the rock, "go on." He drew the Navy Colt. "I shall be within hand's touch of you at your heels. One false move, one whisper of delay, one hint of snuffing the light, and I shall empty the cylinder into you."

"Ghosts!" cried the old man happily. "Down the long black hole to where the shades dwell in old Pegleg's private mountain. Hee hee hee, foller along, Mr. Draco. You will see such things as ain't been see'd by mortal eyes what lived to blink about it afterwards. Hee hee!"

They began the sliding, bumping, rough-floored descent of the crude shaft cut in its incline of thirty degrees to forty-five degrees out of horizontal level. At times Draco literally fell through the mountain. Again, the way would turn upward, sometimes even by crude log ladder, only to pitch away downward again into blackness blinder than the pit. The Executive went where the gleam of Ratsmith's headlamp candle beckoned him. He lost track of time and was startled to hear the madman's voice cackling and laughing, "Hee hee, soon now, friend Draco. Right yonder where you see the shine of the candle picking up the glow. You see it, Draco, you see the glow?"

Draco strained his good eye ahead. His heart, hammering from the exertion of the descent, seemed to speed faster, suffocating life. Great God, Jesus, he *could* see the glow! It was a luminous pulsating cloud-like thing of no earthly origin and no mortal confines. It was the pure color, the heart of the place where it all came from. It was solid gold fired by one small candle's gleam into an entire mountain's flaming heart. It was the bonanza.

Moments later they had stumbled free of the tunnel and were in the golden stope of Pegleg Gates.

Like Ben Allison before him, Selman Draco could not properly absorb the crushing weight of riches beyond the wildest strike story ever lied into legend before that stunned minute in the old prospector's treasure-house.

Draco's mind plunged over the lip of the precipice.

He shouted, wept, cried out a foulness of obscenities into the glittering vault of the place. Like an animal he clawed at the veinings, ripping out the rotten chunky gold of the mother lode by hand. The gold cascaded down in pea gravel, sandgrain, flour and nuggets of grouse-egg-to-turkey-egg size, all the many forms and kinds of the pure color where God had originally stored it to stock a thousand creeks, ledges, pockets, placers, streaks, and smears and wild-rose quartz veins to last a hundred centuries and supply the lives of ten thousand miners with their outside finds.

In God's name, the man who owned this pulsing glow of firelit metal could buy the world.

Selman Draco was that man.

From that moment in that mountain he needed no vigilance committee, no witnesses, no testimonials for the defense. He need only kill the cowboy and the Negro and the wicked harlot with them, and Nathan Stark and Esau Lazarus and the Vigilantes of Montana would never hear a word against the name or honor or

112

the dedicated service of Selman Draco, Executive, Canyon Creek Committee.

Gold could buy the silence of the living.

It could give falsifying tongue to the muted dead.

Selman Draco was free!

In the very instant of his rising, the Executive was met by a reedy chortling voice behind him and even as the unstable chittering of the cripple's "hee hee hee!" struck its chill into his victory, the light of the single candle flicked out.

Selman Draco was a king in an empire of sudden, choking, total blackness.

Ratsmith was gone.

25

Outside the cabin Ben whistled five minutes before his anxious ear caught the return whinny of his Comanche mustang. When the Indian pony loped up from the darkness the tall cowboy gentled him quickly, got Ellie Semple and Ruel Oakes mounted up bareback, and gave the mulatto boy the Kwahadi knee signals for guiding him.

It was an eighteen-mile trip to Virginia City over the Elkhorn Hills shortcut. The night would soon be gone and if lawyer Lazarus was to be fetched back in time the ride must start at once. "Good luck," Ben said, and slapped the mustang on the rump. The little horse took out on the trot, broke into its mile-eating lope, then was swiftly gone from sight in the winter blackness.

Ben turned again to the cabin of Fagan Ratsmith.

Given the surprise of the ambush he figured to set inside for Draco and the returned ghost of Pegleg Gates, the game ought to be over. Ben Allison, of San

Saba, Texas, had his gun back. The man who could beat him with the old .44-caliber tied down where it belonged had not come up the trail yet. The gun was Ben Allison's business and he was back in business.

He flashed the matchless draw, the action triggered by the instinct of the thought. The weapon appeared in the big hand as it always had—invisibly. All right. It was set, then: cutting their sign in the antechamber up at drift head, Pegleg and Draco would have to find that Ruel had taken the gold-stope tunnel, leaving Ben only the problem of waiting for them inside the shack. When they came out of the mountain through that old wooden door, he would stretch Draco with the barrel bent over the back of his head and deal with the crippled prospector in whatever gentle or necessary way might develop. It was in his mind that Pegleg Gates could be reasoned with. The eerie old goat had shown a good heart in cutting a half-Negro boy into the vast treasure of the Ghost Ridge bonanza room. Surely, Ben could make him see that the drifter kid had not meant to give away Pegleg's secret by bringing him and Elvira into the mountain.

Satisfied, the big Texan re-entered the unlit shack. He had no more than done so when his neck hairs arose.

Beyond the wooden door, which on its cabin side was covered skillfully by a nailed-up bearhide, he heard the sudden shuffle and slide of rock which indicated passage of the steep descent tunnel into the cabin.

Ben glided with Comanche silence to the wall beside the bearskin. The long-barreled revolver was out of its leather, poised for the cold-cock which would bring Selman Draco to a fairer justice than he deserved.

The plank door squealed on rusted hangers. The bearhide came away from the wall six inches—and stopped.

The tall gunman tried to blink away the darkness of both cabin and opened door gap, straining also to hear what he could not see. Christ Jesus, nothing. Just the brief sliding of the tunnel rubble, creak of door,

114

and nothing. Ghosts again? No, ghosts did not breathe and now Ben heard breathing, human breathing. And it was not that of a vital man, a Selman Draco, but rather the ticking wheezing of an older man and Ben knew then who waited beyond the bearhide door—but why alone?

Where was Draco if not with Pegleg's ghost called Fagan Ratsmith?

God! Could the demented little cripple have killed the Canyon Creek committeeman, killing with him the last best chance remaining to Ruel Oakes to clear himself of the wrongful charge of the dancehall girl's murder?

Could the warped mind of the strange old man have robbed Ben and Ruel in this bitter way? And robbed the ghost of Billie Dove Vardeen? Did he now intend to add Ben Allison to his madman's list of those who must die because they had seen the blinding glory of the golden stope?

Suddenly, the small and crippled figure of Fagan Ratsmith or of Pegleg Gates was not the simple, second-handed thing it had been. In a pitchy darkness such as Ben now found himself trapped within, a man had better bring light and bring it right swiftly. Blackness of the pit was Pegleg's world—or Ratsmith's musty den. Had it taken Selman Draco and now yawned to suck in Ben Allison?

Ben reholstered the long-barreled Colt, eased back along the wall away from the bearhide, followed the wall completely around the cabin on feet trained by his grandmother's people to whisper not above the rustle of the buffalo grass, scrape no more than the fieldmouse scraped going over a white man's wooden floor.

He came to the bearhide wall again, this time on the side toward which the hidden door stood six inches open.

Gathering himself, he kicked the door wide, leaped into the blackness beyond it, and collided, full-jump, with something human which squealed and bit like a rat and then, when dragged forth into the open of the cabin, commenced to giggle and laugh in a high-pitched, grating "hee hee hee!" that brought the big Texan to drop it with a curse.

"Goddamn you, Pegleg Gates!" Ben said. "You bite me onct again and I will skin you out for coyote bait."

He blinked as a sulphur match was scratched on the floor and Walter J. "Pegleg" Gates crawled out from under his rickety hand-hewn table to light a dish candle on that table and announce matter-of-factly, as if it were high noon and Ben Allison invited for dinner, "Hee hee, don't take it amiss, mister. What would you be doing your ownself if somebody thrict your size flang hisself upon you in the pitch of dark in your own legal-titled domicile?"

"Well, Christ," growled Ben, sucking his wound, "I for certain wouldn't think to be winning with no weasel bites. Where the hell at is Selman Draco?"

"Safe!" chortled the misshapen owner of the golden mountain. "He is where he will keep like a side of beef, even temperature the year around and no light to spoil the cure. Hee hee hee."

"You trapped him inside the hill?"

"You might say, you might say."

"He ain't dead?"

"Not yet." The friendly, hospitable expression vanished. The disfigured face contorted itself unhappily. "You know, stranger," said Pegleg Gates, "I don't recall knowing you. How come you called me what you done called me? Ain't Ratsmith good enough for you?"

In as few words as he might, Ben told him the story of Ruel Oakes from its cruel beginning at the vigilante hearing to the carrying out of sentence at gallows tree flat, the escape from there, return to Canyon Creek— all of it to the moment there in the cabin of Fagan Ratsmith or whoever. "You know, Mr. Gates," Ben concluded, "you done a fine and fitting thing helping that boy like you did. He like to died keeping your secret. Don't you see that? He could have told the town about your big bonanza and they'd have elected him governor of the entire damned territory. Now you think

116

you got to kill him, but you ain't that crazy, Mr. Walter J. Gates."

The little man considered it.

Then shook his head.

"But it's my gold," he said. "I trusted him and he brung in you and the lady. He was my first friend since I got so bad hurt all them years gone, and he turnt on me. He found the gold stope and he led you to it."

"It will be all right," Ben said. "The boy has gone up to Virginia to fetch lawyer Lazarus. We're going to have an open trial on Selman Draco. It was him murdered that dancehall girl and we aim to prove it on him and hang him for it—legal and right. We do that and bust up these-here stranglers for good, and you can come out of your mountain again and be the friend to the whole camp that you once was. With the legal law established in the territory, there ain't nobody can take your gold away, not nobody. Don't you understand that?"

The cripple shook his head. "Stranglers got the law," he said. "No place for old Ratsmith now, no place atall. You've seed to that, you and your friends."

"Old man," Ben said, growing suddenly afraid, "you got to show me where you got Selman Draco. Without him to try, we ain't a case. We all will have to stay in the mountain with you. Surely you don't want that?"

"Stay in the mountain with old Pegleg, hee hee hee. That's a good idee, stranger. Yes, we'll have a hull passel of ghosts—lady ones, nigger ones, Texas reb ones, strangler ones. Hee hee! You got a good mind, boy. Come on, let old Ratsmith show you."

Ben held back.

"Hold up," he admonished. "Do me a favor. Make up your mind if it's to be Ratsmith or Pegleg Gates, will you? A man gets confused."

He said it merely to gain time, to think, to try to figure some way to handle the hunchback and yet get the Vigilance Committee Executive out of Ghost Ridge alive. But the suggestion had point for the demented prospector.

"Of course, of course," he accented at once. "Did

117

you know I was in the theater before I started to hunt for gold? Ah! Them were the days: *Walter John Gates Appearing, Tonight Only, in 'Mazeppah!' Direct from New York and the State Theaters of Imperial Europe!* Oh, but it were grand, boy. Let me show you, let me show you . . ."

He trailed off, going across the cabin to fumble in a shabby pyramid of broken trunks and shipping boxes with strange and far-off labels. Nearby, at an ancient dressing table with shellacked mirror, the cripple seated himself and, before Ben's bugging eyes, peeled away the mat of make-believe hair which covered his face, lumps of padding which made the hunchback and constructed the dragging leg, and going on from these structed the dragging leg, and going on from thes major things to remove swiftly the other sordid costumings of Fagan Ratsmith. While his viewer yet gaped, he hopped over to the iron cookstove and retrieved from its kindling box a wooden leg which he expertly strapped to the stump which had borne the dragging-limb device and was thus, all in the three minutes the dumfounded cowboy stared, once again the Pegleg Gates of ten years gone.

"God almighty," Ben apologized. "Alongside you, Mr. Gates, John Wilkes Booth was a tinplated piker!"

The big Texan applauded with good feeling and the simple honesty which was his. Affected, the little man bowed and bowed and bowed again, pirouetting awkwardly from stage left to stage right of the tumbledown shack.

"Thanks, dear friends. So kind of you all. Thank you, thank you!"

He blew a kiss to the audience of stillness beyond the tall cowboy, the tears of yesterday shining in the candled footlights. "Good night, good night, farewell!"

With the adieu and before Ben might recover from his enchantment, Pegleg swept up a kerosene lantern, lit it from the table candle, and flourished its beacon.

"Come along, pardner," he invited, the theatrical

118

past as swiftly forgotten as sadly recalled. "Yonder is Mr. Draco, old kingpin of the stranglers. I reckon you are dead correct that such as him has got to go to miners' court." He smiled at Ben, shrugging his defeat. "I never truly meant to leave him to die in the dark."

Ben eyed him gratefully.

"You're aiming to light the way, old-timer?"

"You cain't find it otherwise, not and handle him, too. He's mean as a teased dog. Got to have more'n a candle to see your way back out with that one."

"Mr. Gates," Ben said, "you are right as a railroad watch. Lead on, kindly light."

Pegleg cackled his pleasure at the trust, commenced leading the way up the steep tunnel beyond the bearhide door. Going along, he sang a cracked and wobbly version of the hymn Ben had suggested:

> Lead, kindly light
> Amid th' en-cir-cling gloom
> Lead Thou me on
> The night is dark
> And I am far from home . . .
> Lead Thou me on
> Keep Thou my feet
> I do not ask to see the distant scene
> One step is good enough for me—

Ear-wrenching as the singing was, Ben felt uplifted by it. It was an omen surely. Things had been bad for him and old Ruel Oakes, but now it looked to the big Texas cowboy as though he might truly see ahead the light at the end of the tunnel. Pegleg was taking him to Selman Draco. There was no chance the vigilante chieftain was going to get away from Ben or from standing witness to that fair trial in open court which Ben had promised the mulatto boy. Draco was a snake, sure, but being left to soak up all that dark there in the gold stope, thinking he would never again see the light of day, or any light—well, the son of a bitch simply had to be beaten down with sheer gladness

119

to see Ben Allison and Pegleg Gates coming with that glorious kerosene lantern. Ben would herd him back out into the old man's cabin peaceful as a slaughter lamb. There, he would truss him up tighter than a roast Christmas goose, stand guard over him till daybreak, and pack him into Canyon Creek on old Pegleg's firewood sled which he had seen leaning up against the ratty shack's chimney just outside the door.

Why, hell, it was all over but the towing through the snow. He might even get a break on that by using the wagon road to Bozeman. Somebody might come riding along topside of a Murphy or Studebaker flatbed, and agree to haul Draco in for a reasonable charge.

Such are the delights and illusions of the simple in heart and mind.

When, shortly, Pegleg's lantern caught the golden fire of the stope room ahead, and he and Ben Allison had entered the cavern to the rescued Selman Draco's shaken relief and gratitude, it went precisely as Ben had it in his plans. Draco accepted the arrest, permitted Ben to belt-strap his hands together behind his back, vowed he feared no trial in any man's court of legal law, and suggested they get on outside the mountain, forthwith.

Ben, of course, was still watchful. Simple is not the same as stupid.

He was in a lawman's role now, he who had always before been the outlaw. It was an unfamiliar feeling and he was pleased that the Canyon Creek committeeman understood the situation and surrendered to it. But the ill wind was from another way.

Even as he cinched up the last twist of the belt on Draco's hands, there was a stuttering "hee hee hee" from Pegleg Gates and, without further warning than that, the kerosene lantern went out.

"Don't move!" Ben said, jamming his Colt into Draco's spine, but the latter, twisting wildly, broke away and was free in the darkness of the pit and Ben did not fire. Instead, he leaped for where he thought the exit to Pegleg's cabin lay—and slammed with tooth-jarring shock into a flat wall of mother-lode rock.

For his opposite part, a raging Selman Draco rushed through the same blind bat-cave trying also to intercept and bring down the scuttling cripple with the lantern. He, too, collided with the vault's walls, finding no hole and no escape. After a wild moment of cursing and counter-cursing, he and Ben Allison stood in their respective prisons of darkness—bleeding, bruised, beaten.

"Allison," the Executive said, "are you there?"

"No," said Ben, "I'm here."

"Are you on a wall?"

"Yes." Ben scowled, hesitating. "Are you?"

"I am. If one of us goes to his left and the other to his right, we must meet."

"That," Ben agreed, "or one of us find the hole meanwhile. In which case, excuse me, I'm gone."

"No, no. We must stay together. That old devil is going to kill us. We've no choice but to join forces."

"Mebbe. I'll start to my right."

"All right, I'm coming left. No gunplay, Allison."

"I never," Ben assured him, "shoot a man with his hands tied behind his back. Not unless I need to."

He began to move and could hear Draco moving on his farther wall. He had not taken three cautious steps when his reaching boot found empty air against the flat of the wall he was on and he knew what he had found.

"Draco!" he barked. "Cut across straight, follering my voice. Hurry, for Christ's sake. I can hear him digging down there. And singing. Jesus, it's 'Rock of Ages, Cleft for Me!' He's a'going to cave us in here."

"What?" cried the other, falling and stumbling across the great stope room. "What are you saying?"

"I've found the cabin tunnel," Ben called. "I can hear him picking and laughing. Come on, come on—I can see a glimmer of light, way yonder!"

Draco panted up, feeling desperately in the darkness for the wall and for Ben Allison. In the very last moment he, too, saw the faint glimmer of the light far down the cabin tunnel framed between the badly bowed legs of the big Texas cowboy. It was the last sight from that place for either of the men in the golden stope.

"My God!" Ben yelled suddenly. "Get down, get down! I smell fuse smoke!"

With his words, the mountain seemed to heave. Out of the cabin tunnel vomited a screaming cannonade of fire-tortured rock and blast dust. The acrid smell of powder choked lung and throat and nose and for many seconds the debris rained upon Ben and the vigilante leader, then all was again still in the mountain.

There was no sign of light—nor of life—in the treasure hall of Pegleg's sealed bonanza.

26

Ben awoke to the blackness of utter silence. For a moment only his mind groped, then he remembered where he was—or where he had been when Pegleg blew the tunnel.

He felt around himself fearfully as a man will when he truly does not know if he is alive, or dreaming that dream for which there is no ending. The first thing his hand encountered was the body of Selman Draco, and his touch told him Draco was breathing and so must be alive. If Draco, then Ben, he reasoned, and forced his limbs up and out of the immurement of rock shards which held him prisoner to the floor of the golden stope. In a moment he heard Draco groan and, within a short time, had shaken and slapped the Executive back into consciousness.

"You all right?" he asked his companion of the pit.

"God knows," said Draco. "How about you?"

"Never mind," Ben answered, thoughts marshaling more swiftly now. "Listen. We still got us a chanct. Happen neither of us is hurt inside or goes to bleeding, we might make it up the other tunnel to the drift head."

Draco groaned. "I couldn't," he admitted. "Bringing me down here, Ratsmith made a score of false turns and backouts, confusing me. I didn't know why, but when I saw this cavern of mother ore, it was plain—I couldn't find my way back up that tunnel if I had a headlamp. He made certain of that."

"Forget it," Ben said. "My gopher guided us different. He called every twist on the way down, so's me and Ellie Semple could find our ways back up just in case."

The vigilante chieftain stirred. Ben knew he was coming to his feet. "Can you find the tunnel?" he asked.

"Got to," Ben growled. "Here, hold out your hands."

They found each other in the blind darkness and Ben freed the hands of his enemy. He instructed Draco to hold onto the belt, which he looped about his gunbelt, passing the free end to the other man. "It's mad," the latter said. "In this blackness—"

"Shut up and hang on," the big cowboy told him. "I got a little something to show you."

He knew where the upper hole began, having spotted it before Pegleg vanished with the lantern. He went now directly to it and entered. He crawled perhaps ten feet straight along, halted, and fumbled along the wall of the tunnel with both hands. The next thing Draco heard was the scratch of a sulphur match, and he winced at the glare of the tiny flame. Then Ben exclaimed, "Aha! Shit, I knew old Ruel wouldn't miss," and the strangler leader saw the wall niche which held the cached headlamp and its fresh candle. "This here," he said to Draco, donning the lamp and lighting its wick, "is how mulatto niggers repays prominent white citizens what accuses them false of murders they ain't

123

did. Think about that and don't let go the end of the belt; let's crawl, Mr. Vigilante of Montana."

Draco said nothing; it was not in his kind to be grateful for the weaknesses of others, except where that weakness gave Selman Draco a chance where no chance had seemed to exist. In the present case it was not the foresight of Ruel Oakes caring for his white friends that excited the crawling strangler. It was the fact of big Ben Allison's stupid charity of forgiving and helping out even a man he knew to be his deadly avowed enemy. Finding the headlamp, leading the way up and out of the stope tunnel to drifthead and freedom again—ah, these were the true gifts of whatever gods cared for the Selman Dracos of the world. The idiot. He was as good as dead right then. Draco's hands were free. He still had the Navy Colt inside his waistband and it still held one unfired round in its cylinder. The Texas drifter was done for.

Upward, upward, they followed the snakings of Pegleg Gates' fantastic diggings. Ben did not falter nor did the man following him. There was little talk and none needed. Both understood that a third factor beyond either of themselves raced them for the surface outlet high on Ghost Ridge. Ben had named it as they began their desperate climb through the mountain.

"Listen," he told the doubting Executive, "*I* thought of it, didn't I? You think I'm smarter than that old ringy coot yonder? He'll be going for the top, too. Only on the outside of the ridge. If he beats us to the drifthead—"

"Yes, yes!" Draco had gasped. "Keep going."

"You bet I will," Ben vowed. "The way this tunnel lies up there at the drift, a pound of powder and a two-inch fuse would choke the bore for us till Christ came back and died a natural death."

"Goddamn you, be quiet. Climb. Watch the light."

"Yes sir," Ben said. "Sorry." He went on a few feet, then added, "You know, Mr. Draco, that old Peg has got us all figured. Me and you buried alive in the mountain, and him still keeping his gold stope to himself. Then he'll figure a way to quieten old Ruel and

124

Ellie, even after they win their trial, why, Sweet Jesus, you'd ought to have made *him* Executive. No offense, naturally."

He could hear Draco's teeth grinding behind him, but the vigilante leader only said, "The man's criminally insane, Allison. You don't commence to understand him. Earlier tonight, I saw him shoot three men in the back, and then two of them through the head when they weren't quite dead. Johnson, Fleeger, Jack Spain— my best men. Your 'old Peg' murdered them all."

Ben nodded back through the candlelit murk.

"Was it him," he said, "who beat out the brains of Billie Dove Vardeen with Ruel Oakes' camp-ax?"

It was after that that the climb got quiet and the words scarce and that both men knew what they knew.

And it was then, too, that Selman Draco understood he had to kill Ben Allison inside the Old Glory Mine, no matter what crazy Ratsmith-Pegleg might do to both of them with his blasting powder and black fuse.

It was something more than two hours later that big Ben called thankfully back to him, "Drift ahead, Mr. Draco. I can see the pink of outside daybreak against the black of this-here stope tunnel. Keep a'coming."

Draco slid out the Navy Colt.

"I'm coming, Allison," he said.

27

They came up out of the stope tunnel blinking and coughing to clear the rock dust and the bat-blindness of the lower hole from their eyes. From the Old Glory's drift exit to outer ore-dump, they caught

125

the sight of winter sky reddening to sunrise. "Morning!" Ben cried. "Christ Jesus, but that looks good!"

Draco did not answer and too late Ben whirled upon his prisoner. He came around only far enough to see the Navy Colt out and aimed point-blank at his head from behind. Then the gun flashed and roared in the narrow drift and Ben saw a thousand lights brighter than the outside sun. After that came a sightless time and the Canyon Creek Executive cursed and threw away the Navy Colt and stepped to bend over the fallen, motionless body of Ben Allison. Pulling the cowboy's .44-caliber from its holster, he put the muzzle of the long barrel to Ben's head, cocking back the spur hammer, eyes glaring wildly.

"Goddamn your soul to hell," he said coldly, and tightened his finger on the trigger.

But something stayed the fatal pressure.

It was a sound of familiar music out upon the ore-dump's farther side. The song was not the same, but the singer was. And Selman Draco froze, confused.

> Work for the night is coming
> Work through the morning hours
> Work while the dew is sparkling
> Work mid springing flowers

Draco's concerned snarl made no sound. He stepped away from Ben, the bad eye bulging, neck veins swollen to twig-thick ridges. That bastard, that crazy old son of a bitch, he thought. Now, he had to come just now. Why—why?

> Work for the night is coming
> Work through the sunny noon

The Executive ran stumblingly for the drift exit, the tall man's cavalry Colt still cocked in his hand. The demented old devil must die. He must not witness Selman Draco again at murder, nor must he be permitted to blow the upper tunnel and put the stope of gold forever beyond the reach of the man who would

126

buy Montana with its treasure, should that indeed prove his present mission. Time would remain in plenty for Ben Allison. Yes, yes, surely so. But here was the timber framing of the entrance. Be careful, Selman. Show yourself, but not the gun. Chance must not warn the victim. Just so, now, just so.

The strangler chieftain paused, and took a steadying breath.

> ... Work in the glowing sun
> Work for the night is coming
> When man's work is done—

Selman Draco stepped from the mine drift into view of the full dump. To his left came the old man, hauling his firewood sledge by frayed rope, toiling inward over the snow-clad tailings of his monumental borings within the great ridge of Ghost Hill. But the sledge did not bear kindling sticks or handhewn cords of pine. Instead, its lone cargo was composed of a black cannister labeled, in yellow stencil, DUPONT'S BEST HERCULITE STUMP AND ROCK, #4 BLACK BLASTING, a half coil of shiny fast-running fuse, and an ancient percussion double-barreled shotgun so rusted as to proclaim even from afar its uselessness.

"Ho!" called the crippled prospector, resting his wooden leg upon the sledge. "Who be thar? Friend or foe, don't make no difference. Ye're trespassin', damn you. Hold right whar you be."

He reached for the rusted smoothbore and Draco fired with the big .44-caliber from the hip. He was not accustomed to either the feel of Ben's trigger or to the recoil of the heavy weapon. His shot missed the old man by an inch, hit behind him, and ricochetted screaming off over the dump's deep fall into the canyon below.

Pegleg dove for the rear of the wood sledge, down behind his load of blasting powder. Draco fired the entire cylinder of Ben's gun between the time of the first shot and the arrival of the old man's face into the snow behind the sledge. The last shot, following the

127

oldster, actually hit the crimped heavy rim of the black cannister of powder. It, too, was a ricochet, but one with a difference.

Sweating instantly, Draco lowered the smoking Colt. Good Jesus, he could have blown up the whole dump, the old devil, and himself with it.

Now he had alerted Pegleg and had him on the prod out there with an ancient outside-hammered birdgun which just might work and just might be loaded with something better than birdshot—say number-two duck and goose.

The Executive wheeled back into the drift, racing for the body of the silent cowboy. Ripping away Ben's gunbelt, Draco swung it about his own waist, buckled it down, ran again for the entrance, reloading the big Colt as he went. He intended to make a dash for the drifthead shack and the tailings-crushing mill out on the dump's end. From there, he would have the angle of fire to get at the old man nor could the latter reach him effectively with the shotgun on the dash. He might get pinked by a stray shot or two, but they would be fading with distance and of no threat. Pegleg Gates would be a ghost at last.

The assumption nearly proved to be the last of mortal flesh for Selman Draco.

Pegleg had not waited cringed behind his sledge, but had charged his legal-owned minehead the instant Draco had drawn back into the drift. In consequence the range, when the Executive broke from the drift for the dump-end buildings, was about a good grouse shot. The thunder of the crippled prospector's antique piece shook snow from the lintel and header timbers of the drift's entrance. Lead shot splashed entrance-frame joists, threshold floor, and the near rock of the tunnel's lip and throat, but Selman Draco, sprinting behind the blur of shotshell smoke and dislodged snow, gambled for his life and won, getting cleanly away from the drift. Pegleg's second barrel was poorly aimed and fired, serving only to throw up more snowdust and more gunpowder stink as it chaperoned the Executive into the nearby buildings.

Yet the owner of the Old Glory was not entirely outmatched.

As Draco ran so did Walter J. Gates go haltingly, ahop on his wooden leg, but with surprising speed to get behind the shattered trunk of a specimen pine thrown down from the slope above by an avalanche eight years before.

Here, halfway between drift head and ore dump-end, he took shelter and happily began to recharge the chambers of his vintage smoothbore goose-gun.

It was this scene upon which Ben Allison, roused up from unconsciousness by the shattering explosion of Pegleg's shotgun, tottered weakly forth from the drift of the Old Glory Mine. Draco's murderous shot had glanced on hard Texas skullbone, the small .36-caliber ball of the Navy Colt failing its deadly mission. Ben was still in the fight, if somewhat bloodied and pale. He was, in fact, cheerfully greeted by Pegleg upon appearance.

"Hee-yah thar, stranger! Hee hee! We got us a damn piebald claim jumper cornered in the shack yonder— come along on and help me to smoke him out!"

"Draco?" Ben guessed, head still cotton-thick.

His answer came with the boom of his own .44-caliber Colt fired from the shack. Still dazed, his hand slapped the emptiness at his side. Two slugs from the outer dump ripped through his shirt before he recovered and lurched back into the drift. Groaning, he braced himself along the wall.

Now what? God knew, he had to get back out there, had to somehow cross that dump and get to Selman Draco. Then take him unharmed prisoner—not angrily gun him down.

Think, Ben, he thought. First the dump. How do you cross it?

My God, there it was, the answer—right in the anteroom of the drift. Ruel and the old man had jury-rigged a windbreaker for their stone fireplace; it was the bottom steel plate of a one-mule drag scraper used to level the dump. Ben could muscle it up and carry it, and this he proceeded to do.

129

He came out of the drift behind it and on the bent run so unexpectedly that he was halfway to Pegleg's fort behind the down pine before Draco opened up.

Then it was like Saturday night at the traveling carnie show with the rubes laying down their dimes to knock over those iron ducks and the lead flying like all hell yet hitting nothing but those tin mallards—*whang! abang! cal-lang!*—and just plain *plink* when they missed one and hit the zinc-plate backstop. But Draco didn't miss; he hit the scraper six-for-six of the shots he threw. If they had been in Dallas or Fort Worth, he would have won the Kiowa Indian doll or the hand-painted Dresden chamber pot for sure. But it was still Montana and Ben, after reaching Pegleg's side, was not whooping it up in his natural Texas style as he had been coming across the dump behind the scraper. His head was, in fact, bleeding heavily again and he only got it stopped with the old man's help in tying it off tight with an heirloom "Red Dot" bandanna which had not seen the washtub since the flood of 1856.

No matter, goddamnit.

Ben Allison was out there behind the pine log with the daft galoot, they had a ten-gauge shotgun to share, and they had Selman Draco boxed in the ore-dump tailings shack.

It was time to thank the good Lord and to take a deep breath before the next long jump. Well, almost.

Ben heard the warning clink of the shotgun's outside hammers being pulled back to full cock by the old miner and his gunman's instincts told him precisely what was happening, yet froze him where he was, regardless—with his back to Pegleg Gates and the ten-gauge.

"Old-timer," he said desperately, "I'm your friend."

"Got no friends," denied the old man. "Turn around. I ain't going to shoot nobody in the shoulder-blades."

"Ease the hammer down," pleaded Ben.

"You seen the gold, stranger; turn about slow."

Ben understood that death and life now hung for

him with the tick of the clock of time running in the sick old mind behind him. He did not turn slow, but with a screech and a diving roll to the ground that knocked down his executioner in the same instant that the right-hand barrel roared. Ben's ears rang and for five seconds he could not see for powderburn and smoke sting. But *he* had the shotgun in one hand and the old man's wooden leg in the other. And as the old rascal now came up spitting snow and ore chips from the dump, Ben struck him over the stubborn skull with the come-loose pegleg, putting him to peaceful, quiet, and convenient sleep.

Folding the old bastard's hands about the detached leg as though it were a lily, Ben placed the wooden limb on the breast of Walter J. Gates, said something unkind as to his mother, and then turned back. His pale eyes were narrowed now and any cowboy spirit was long since quieted, upon the grim, final business of Selman Draco's taking.

He raised up the drag scoop's metal and stood behind it and behind the down pine.

"Draco," he called with a soft chilling drawl, "you remember what you said in the tunnel when I called out to you light was ahead? Well, it's broad day, Draco, and I'm a'telling you the same thing."

He picked up the shotgun and braced the iron scraper.

"Get set," he said. "I'm a'coming."

28

Pegleg Gates tottered up to lean against the downed pine log, thoughts fogging. Remembering his enemies, he limped unsteadily over the dump to its outer ending and was in time to see two figures climb-

131

ing the scaffolded rigging of the tailings mill known in Canyon Creek as "Old Walt's Coffee Grinder." More seasons gone than he now recalled, the old man had dreamed to mill dry ore with a special giant granite burr turned on cast-steel bearings. The millstone had broken up the low-grade ore he was then into, but his weird chute device—a great wooden flume jutting out and over the dump's end—designed to work like a dry riffle-box, dropping various chunks through appropriate screens as the "ground ore" cascaded down the channel of the chute, had failed totally. Its skeletal reminder, the rickety chute tower and the precipitous flume itself, was only another of the burdens of public derision Pegleg had borne through the years of his digging into Ghost Hill and the Old Glory Mine.

Now, he looked up through blurring eyes, focusing to recognize the climbers in his tower. He could not seem to remember them. One, nearing the very top and the hopper which fed down into the chute, was gaunt and suffered from a baleful bulging of one eye. He wore a belted buscadero rig of Texas origin and cursed aloud as he scrambled to escape his pursuer. The latter was also a gaunt fellow but of even stranger dress and carrying for a weapon, which slowed his climbing severely, a double-barreled shotgun.

"Hyar, hyar!" the old man heard himself screeching. "I'll have the law onto you both. This here is private propetty, you damned rascals. Come down off my mill!"

But the climbers did not hear him or, if hearing, did not heed him. Even as his words wailed into the winter morning's stillness, the second man stopped and hooked a bowed leg for bracing and blasted upward at his quarry with the shotgun. The charge of heavy buckshot tore away a complete four-by-four corner timber just beneath the upper man, almost precipitating him down upon the snowy rock of the dump. But he held on and even returned fire with his big Colt revolver, scattering wood shards all about the tall man who clung below him.

Then they were climbing again and the higher man

saw that the lower one had gained in under the chute and knew he yet had the second barrel of the terrible charge of number-two fowling shot, big as small ball bearings, being held to shred the life out of his enemy when he himself gained the higher edge of the flume and could fire down it.

Pegleg saw the lower man's advantage in the same instant and for reasons unknown to himself gave a whinnying shout of encouragement to the shotgun carrier. His cry seemed but to spur the latter and to convince the man up on the chute hopper that the last chance loomed for him.

Indeed, neither the lower climber nor the ancient mine owner down upon the ore-dump had imagined a last choice existed up there on top of the tailings tower.

The crazed man with the bad eye saw it differently.

With a scream of defiance, he leaped downward into the snow-choked hopper. There was but an instant's delay before his body plummeted through the snow plug in the hopper. Then it burst into view, bombarding and bobsledding down the ice and snow-glazed gullet of the wooden flume. It spewed off the end of the chute far above the slope of the dump, but such was its momentum from the ricochetting ride down the roof-steep pitch of the flume that it struck the slope on a glancing angle. Cartwheeling wildly, the figure of the jumper disappeared down the slope amid a minor slide of ore rock and snow. Limping to the edge of the ore-car platform, Pegleg leaned out over its rail and saw the man's body crash into the brush of Big Canyon Creek far, far below. He was still leaning out over the platform rail when he heard a second body thudding and careering down the overhead of the tailings chute. He crouched instinctively, as the tall form of the pale-eyed stranger with the double-barreled shotgun flew from chute's end to follow the down-slope bounding and tumbling of the first man's body.

The second one did not get the same long ride down the dump as the first, however. His close following of

133

the first jumper apparently disturbed the lay of the dump under its sheath of snow, and an avalanche of ice and tailings broke free to engulf him entirely. Although the old man peered from above for many seconds, he never did see the second body emerge into the clear or reach the creek timber at the bottom deeps.

The peculiar violence of his enemies' ending, however, seemed to rally the old miner's memory, to return him to what it was that had brought him toiling around the mountain with his firewood sledge and his black can of blasting powder. "Yes, yes," he said aloud. "Glory be, glory be." And he began again to sing as he limped across the ore-dump wavering and jolting on the wooden leg.

> Work till the last beam fad—eth
> Fad-eth to shine no more
> Work till the last beam fad-eth
> When man's work is o'er—

Retrieving the sledge, Pegleg went on with it into the portals of his haunted mine. There he unloaded the powder and fuse, rolling the sinister cannister through the anteroom of the drift to the mouth of the down-stope tunnel. Then he carried the container down into the descending shaft a distance of fifty feet. He used no candle, but when he had come precisely as far as he wished he lit a match and the candle was there in its niche in the mother rock of the tunnel and he lighted its wick.

Working the can's lid free, he carefully poured the powder into holes long since prepared in the rock walls. Tamping the grains, he inserted cut fuses, and poured and tamped more powder about them. When all was ready, he merely took up the candle, lit the fuses, and clambered back up the incline to the main drift, singing his hymns again. There was no sadness in his song, now, but rather a lilt of something finally done —even if not soundly.

When the charges blew, the fractured rock spewed back up the stope tunnel, knocking the old prospector

134

flat and battering him with its rain of refuse and choking dust. Peering through the powder smoke, Pegleg coughed and said to the reeking drift, "The Lord gives and the Lord taketh away. She's done. The Old Glory's gone. Glory to God alone. What's His'n is His'n forever, and amen to His gold in this mountain. Walter John Gates has found His truth."

He got up from his knees, his mind, ill so long and so lonely, as of that moment restored. He looked upward for a final time and, with the rock still moving beneath his feet from the upheaval that had sealed the down-stope tunnel, said, in a miner's plain way: "Thank God, she's deep enough for me at last."

When Walter J. "Pegleg" Gates trudged away from the Old Glory that winter's morning in old Montana, there remained but one more mission for him in that place. He had, in his illness, wronged good people and stout friends and these things must be made right again. He would go down to the camp, now, and tell them in Canyon Creek what he had seen there in the alleyway where Billie Dove lived and what he knew from his own eyes of the camp-ax of the mulatto boy Ruel Oakes and, when he had testified all fair and legal to a court of miners like himself, the people would know the truth and it would make them free.

"Glory!" he cried out to the sun and the snow and the deep green pines of the mountain morning. "Glory!"

He set off down the long slope to the mining camp below, wooden leg removed and held aloft, the better to coast on his backside all the way to the bottom.

135

29

Old Kadih, the Kwahadi god of Ben's Comanche grandmother, finally caught up with his quarterblood grandson as the rockslide bore Ben down the high ore-dump toward seeming certain death or maiming in rocky Big Canyon Creek far below. The slide fanned out halfway to the bottom, releasing the big Texan from its granite tomb. He was carried the remainder of the way in a tongue of soft snow which deposited him, unharmed, just short of the creekbed timber.

Kadih did even better than that.

The place where Ben stopped and finally fought free of the snowy debris of the slide was but scant yards from where Selman Draco's glass-clear line of footprints disappeared into that same creek timber. It could not have been over a full minute since the Executive "lit running," as Ben put it. He was up and going for the cover of the stream's brush himself even as the thought hit him.

The timing was close.

Three revolver shots of heavy caliber boomed nearby. The first one struck a snow-laden spruce bough above Ben's head, dislodging a burst of feathery snow which made aiming of the follow-up two shots a matter of blind snap-shooting. Ben survived to get in under cover unhurt. But he had trouble beyond trouble, regardless.

The damned vigilante honcho was not over twenty-five yards away. He knew where Ben was and Ben did not know where he was. He had Ben's gun and Ben's cartridge belt and Ben had a rusty old shotgun jammed full of snow and only one barrel loaded, anyway.

He laughed at himself for having clung to the old weapon all the wild way down the ore-dump.

It was a wonder it hadn't gone off and killed him.

Now here he was huddled like a hunted cottontail in a brushclump, afraid to stay, afraid to run—dead if he moved and dead if he didn't.

But Ben had forgotten something, a weapon that Selman Draco could not have. He thought of it now. And beneath the long flaxen hair the pale gray eyes burned glowingly like slanted coals above the high cheekbones set in the dark skin of the tall man's lean face. He was one-quarter Kwahadi Comanche, a blood grandson of the Water Horse Band. The white man didn't live who could beat him at a stalk-and-kill in dense cover at close quarters.

Ben discarded the shotgun by the simple process of hammer-throwing it up and over his brushy covert in the general direction of Draco's previous fire burst. The heavy weapon flew silently until it struck into the alder and spruce forty feet away. Draco, nerves raw, fired three more shots into the blind noise of the shotgun's fall.

Under cover of the fire's thunder, Ben ran lightly to his left, finding new refuge in a boulder pile which flanked the Executive's position and was twenty feet closer in to him. Only silence greeted him, however.

Draco had correctly judged the ruse of the thrown shotgun. He would not again fire blindly at noise or movement; if Ben were to take him now it would be only when he, Ben, exposed himself plainly by overt attack. The Texan understood this. He crouched amid the boulders of the creekbed, assessing the dilemma.

He counted back on Draco's shots with the Colt .44, since he had taken it from its unconscious wearer. He had now emptied at least two full cylinders. There had been a full cylinder and fourteen spares in the belt when Ben lost the gun, making twenty rounds. Take twelve from twenty and Draco had eight rounds left. And that would be less whatever rounds he may have spent before Ben came around up in the Old Glory

137

drifthead. He might have two, five, three, eight. He was getting low by any counting. All right.

It was time for some Comanche arithmetic.

Behind his boulder pile, Ben seized and muscled down to earth by brute exertion a supple ten-foot sapling of aspen, a wood which would not break under the severe arcing which resulted. Wedging the free end of the small tree into the base of his boulder fortress, he achieved an angle of "aim" with his crude Indian launcher which brought the frost of his quick grin to dark lips.

He stripped off his outer clothing quickly: coat, shirt, Stetson, high Texas boots. The impression Draco would have imprinted on his bulging bad eye would be so brief, and moving so swiftly, that it must be complete in its principal components. The Executive's good eye must "see" black hat, shirt-as-pants, Indian buffalohide jacket, Texas stovepipe drover's boots—the things that would register instant Texas as against familiar Montana to the crazed vigilante leader.

The body was twisted together with bundles of long, winter creekbed grass which was tough, wiry, and perfect for forming. Over this went the clothing, held in its precarious place by bark strips silently peeled from the year-round green of the aspen itself. When all was as ready as Ben Allison could manufacture it according to his quarter-Comanche memory, the tall cowboy made an imprecatory sign skyward to Kadih and stood up in sudden full view of the enemy.

In the precise instant, and as Draco snap-fired from his cover not thirty-five feet distant, Ben kicked at the rock-wedged end of his catapult with total effort.

It nearly broke his bootless foot, but it worked.

The steel-spring sapling came free with an explosive slingshot whip which sent the spurious figure hurtling out from behind the boulder pile on a low-bounding course. It appeared as the real Ben ducked back down or rather, in actual fact, was slammed back down by the second of Draco's two snapped shots caroming the ribs of his left side. But the bruising smash was well risked.

138

Selman Draco reacted instantly to the seeming lunge of big Ben Allison—lurching wildly from the hit Draco knew he had scored on his enemy—out from behind the boulder pile and vanishing with a spectacular head-first splash into the icy waters of Big Canyon Creek. The Executive leaped like an animal from his own covert, charging the wounded prey up to the very edge of the stream. He was still snarling, still pumping the last four rounds of the Colt .44 into the back of Ben's buffalohide coat, when the tall rider came soundlessly across the snow behind him.

Like blacksmith Jensen at gallows tree flat, Selman Draco remembered only the iron forearm sliding into its crushing bar across his throat from the rear.

And after that came blackness.

30

It is the way of dangerous trails that when they turn away at last from peril, the path is swift to straighten.

When Ben Allison brought Selman Draco, disarmed and bound, captive from the creek timber beside the Virginia City Wagon Road, he was met by a committee from that camp bound into Canyon Creek. The men were ten in number, all well mounted, stern, and even grim of visage. Their leader was known by sight to Ben but not in person—F. X. Reedler, head of the parent Virginia Vigilantes. Reedler greeted the lanky cowboy with practiced ease.

"You will be Allison, the Texas drover," he said. "I assume you have placed your prisoner in a citizen's arrest and are taking him into Canyon Creek."

"Yes," Ben said watchfully. "This here is Selman

Draco, Executive of the vigilantes down this way. I charge him with murder." He did not know if the vigilante headman intended to force Draco's release, and so let his hand drop low to brush the worn walnut of the Colt .44's butt. "I mean to see him tried in open miners' court, fair and legal."

Reedler nodded.

"We mean the same."

"For certain sure?" Ben said.

"Walk him ahead of us down the middle of the road," said F. X. Reedler. "My men and I will follow." He waved to the others, nodded once more to the still-delaying Ben. "It's all right. We know your circumstance. Esau Lazarus is already in Canyon Creek with your friends, or should be by this time. We are down from Virginia to see final justice done. You have my word on it."

"I will take it, Mr. Reedler," Ben said gratefully.

They went on into town—a curious, silent cavalcade in the mid-morning sunshine. When Ben had his prisoner up to the camp jail, he found ready friends— editor Harriman, Frenchy Burloign, blacksmith Jensen, and no less than a dozen of the former hanging posse— to receive Draco and prepare him for the court, announced for that same noon only an hour hence. By the time he had looked up Ruel Oakes and Ellie Semple and heard their stories of the night ride to Virginia and Alder Gulch, the rough-garbed miners had gathered in the Masonic Hall down from the Blue Light Livery Barn and next to the Oriental Saloon. Ben, Ruel, and Ellie were taken inside and given witness seats. The judge, down from Virginia with Esau Lazarus, proved a welcome, bright surprise for Ben Allison.

"It's the United States Government," he said excitedly to Ruel and Ellie. "That's old Judge Larned Handelmann as tried me up to Bozeman. How come he's here, you reckon?"

Ellie leaned over, whispering across Ruel Oakes.

"He was visiting with lawyer Lazarus. They were meeting on the vigilante problem. Seems the judge got wind of the way they blue-ticketed you right on his courthouse steps. He didn't care for it a damned bit, lawyer Lazarus says. You really started something, cowboy."

"Hell," denied Ben, "it wasn't me. It was old Ruel here. This here's *his* trial, by God."

The mulatto boy looked at him and seemed embarrassed but mightily glad, too. "Thank you, Mr. Ben," was all he could muster by way of acknowledgment.

Ben grinned, squeezed Ruel's knee, and winked.

"Don't you mention it, Mr. Ruel," he answered. "Rear up on your hindlegs like you had some good sense," he added sternly. "Yonder comes His Honor to the bench."

The flag of the United States was brought in and stuck, propped up, in an empty hogshead in one corner. The sixteen-member jury filed in from the street and took their places on two long plank benches. The bailiff, freshly arrived from the Oriental, rapped for order in the court with the butt of his single-shot horse pistol.

"Hear ye! Hear ye!" he bawled in whiskey-hoarse tones. "This court of the people, County of Canyon Creek, Territory of Montana, be now in session. We got us a U.S. of A. judge all the way from Bozeman, and there ain't going to be no funny business, now nor hereafter. Court's in session."

"You already said that," yelled one of the spectators from the jammed doorway to the hall.

"You're goddamned right I did!" shouted back T. C. Ogden, the bailiff, and corresponding secretary of the Masons in Canyon Creek. "That's so hammerheads like you will understand it straight. Order up, by God, or stand outside!"

The crowd laughed and quieted down all at one time.

Judge Handelmann arose and made a short speech.

A time had come in Montana Territory, he said, when the law must be one law; the day of the riders for popular justice was done and it remained for the people of the territory to make that understood in terms which could not be confused. In that very hall on that very morning the beginning could be made.

It was while the judge was speaking that Ben noted the ominous filing in through the mob at the street door of a second, unannounced jury. It consisted of ten members and a foreman—the Virginia Vigilance Committee, with famed F. X. Reedler in command. An uneasy and vibrant buzzing ran through the packed benches of the meeting hall when their arrival became noted. Judge Handelmann, a fellow little if any less forbidding of mien than Reedler, did not miss the supplementary veniremen from the mother camp. He did not permit it to influence his composure or his plea.

"Let the court note," he said, staring eye to eye with F. X. Reedler, "the presence of the hearing committee from Virginia. And let the record show that the court understands the gentlemen are not in attendance for any reason other than to observe the very necessity for a single law which has led this court to convene in Canyon Creek on this date in the month of February."

Esau Lazarus, a balding dignified Jewish scholar respected the territory over, arose.

"The prosecution so notes," he said.

"Very well," nodded Larned Handelmann. "Who appears for the defendant, Selman Draco?"

Draco, white as the outside snows, stood up from his chair placed before the judge's table and flanked by the jury's twin benches. "Selman Draco defends himself," he said. "Let the record show it."

"You are entitled to counsel, Mr. Draco," Handelmann reminded him.

"I have counsel," Draco said proudly. "My degree is in law, *Juris Doctor,* the University of Virginia, sir, class of '57."

Esau Lazarus broke in softly. "Summa cum Laude," he said.

142

"Magna cum Laude," corrected the other. "And thank you, sir. Defendant is prepared."

Testimony commenced and was not overlong.

That of Mrs. Elvira Semple, Harriman, Jensen, Burloign, and the various members of the hanging posse went as might be assumed and without incident. The witness of the young mulatto lad, Ruel Oakes, was another matter.

It was not testimony in the proper sense but rather a stating of origins more poignant and important to the case than many a labored item of prima-facie proof.

His name, the Negro youth began, was taken from that of his white father, a wealthy young Mississippi plantation owner. His mother was a slave girl of but fifteen years of age, Ruel's own age that day in far Montana. When the young master, only sixteen himself at the time of fathering the half-blood boy, went away to the great war, he was still but twenty-four, a young hero much loved by all who served him, black and white. But when the war was partway over, the young master came home with a terrible head wound, a wound which disfigured his handsome looks and, worse by far, sickened his fine mentality and happy nature. Upon recovery, he was not the same human being, but a dangerous and brutal creature of violence.

Still not thirty years of age, he had killed a man in senseless cold blood and been forced to flee the South for his very life, not being seen again at Drakehurst, the family home near Chupelo, on the big river.

Ruel's mother, already ill, worsened and died when the master disappeared. On her last night, she had charged young Ruel to travel on away from the home place and find his rightful father. He was to tell him who he was and who his mother had been, Tiyanna, the Ghanian girl. Then, she knew, he would welcome Ruel and make a place for him and care for him in his new life.

In this way, the mulatto boy told the crowded courtroom in Mason's Hall, his mother promised him he would find his freedom.

He had been nearing thirteen, then.

For three long years he had followed the trackline of the master of Drakehurst from frontier settlement to frontier settlement, finding him at long and happy last in this very camp of Canyon Creek in far Montana Territory.

At this point the boy paused a long time, looking at Selman Draco, who would not return his mute appeal.

"Ain't no need to tell you," Ruel spoke at last to the silent jury and the rapt courtroom, "yonder's my father, though he won't confess it no more now, I reckon, than when I came here seeking for to find him." Again the painful pause, the long journey back through the years. "You call him Mr. Draco," the mulatto boy said low-voiced. "When we knowed him, it were Selman Oakes and all of us loved him dearly."

The lad sat down, unable to continue.

Indeed, his story was done.

"Your last witness, please, counselor," Larned Handelmann called to Esau Lazarus, and the gentle Jew declined and said softly, "Will defense not examine then, sir?"

Selman Draco would not reply, only looking off over the heads of the silent miners, and the judge directed Lazarus to continue.

"Prosecution calls Mr. Walter J. Gates," said Lazarus in the same soft voice, yet the words could not have had a greater effect than a drift-face explosion.

Walter Gates?

Pegleg Gates?

The ghost of the Old Glory Mine?

The room broke into a babble, a surge to see who might possibly come forth in answer to this daft call by Nathan Stark's attorney.

At the door there was a cry and the people gave back to make a way. Through that cleared path, up to the bar of justice, limped Pegleg Gates, wooden limb thumping hollowly on the board floor of the dead-still hall.

"I'm Walter J. Gates," he piped in the reedy voice

144

which had been Fagan Ratsmith's. "Be damned if I ain't."

"We believe you," Handelmann assured him. "Please tell your story, Mr. Gates. Quiet in the courtroom!"

Pegleg, after a false start or two, a break in the voice, a lump in the throat, the things that come with seeing old friends again, got to his testimony. It was not legally precise, nor ramblingly long, but it devastated any last hope of Selman Draco.

In sum, the old prospector, as Fagan Ratsmith, had been in the drifthead anteroom on the day Draco, hunting deer on the ridge, came in from the cold and, thinking no one home, warmed himself and went on—taking with him the cheap camp-ax of the mulatto boy, Ruel Oakes.

He, Pegleg, had followed the vigilante leader out of the curiosity this strange theft aroused in him. The trail took him to the alley behind the Blue Light Barn and the Oriental Saloon, to the bawdyshack of Billie Dove Vardeen. Hiding in the barn's root cellar, the old man had peeped beneath its trap door and seen what he had seen and what he now swore was the truth: Selman Draco going into the girl's house with the ax of Ruel Oakes and coming back out of the house but moments later without the mulatto youth's ax and going furtively to a nearby bank of dirty old snow to wash his hands in a vast hurry and anxious state.

When he had gone on to enter the Oriental, Pegleg, again as Ratsmith, had crept to the snowbank and found fresh red blood in the place where Selman Draco had laved and scrubbed his hands. He had covered up the terrible sign and later forgotten to report it to anyone, or feared to do so, because of the stranglers and their kind.

Draco leaped from his chair crying the monstrous lie in all of this but, when he was restrained, Pegleg limped over to him and all grew suddenly still.

"Iffen it's hard proof ye want, Mr. Draco," he admonished squeakingly, "leave us all ride out to whar Little Big Canyon dives inter the mountain. Court kin

145

dig out the lead in them three bodies in the snow out thar, commencing with the three bullets in the head of Selkirk Johnson, same whicht ye fired inter his skull whiles he lay unconscious in the oat bin yonder to the Blue Light."

Again Draco began to shout and fight his guards.

"All the same," said the old man. "Court will find one more each in the bodies of Fleeger and Spain, with a extry one in the mouth of old Fat, who wouldn't quit fussing over his luck. And all of that thar lead come out'n a Colt's Navy revolver, and will be caliber .36 balls, all of a match to Mr. Draco's fine piece."

The court stood adjourned on that climax.

A committee of manhunters of experience, led by Frenchy Burloign, was dispatched to fetch back the evidence of the bodies and the dug-out balls which had killed them. It was late in the day before all was in evidence and court again convened. Sentence followed examination of the exhibits.

"Selman Oakes, sometime known as Draco," Judge Handelmann intoned, "this jury finds you guilty in the first degree of murder most foul and heinous, and remands you in custody this same night for transport to imprisonment in the territorial jurisdiction, Bozeman, where you will be held pending execution of sentence. Court adjourned."

It was 5:00 P.M., nearing full darkness.

The trial of Ruel Oakes and Ben Allison was over, but the ending of Selman Draco was not.

A higher court than that of Larned Handelmann and the sixteen-man miners' jury of Canyon Creek had decided that before the bailiff's gavel fell.

31

The people of the camp came later that evening and in small number to the home and blacksmith shop of Dansk Jensen to see or speak with the Texas gunfighter and the Mississippi mulatto lad who had that day added their names to Montana's pioneer roster.

Ben, busy with Jensen preparing to depart with daybreak for Texas and the southern sun, saw at once that the well-wishers were not at ease.

They behaved as if afraid to be seen there.

As if they might subsequently be called to account for being kind to a Texas cowherd and a nigger kid.

As he and the blacksmith worked loading Dansk's snug Murphy freight wagon against the long journey, and as the curious drew apart and permitted the brief chances to talk in guarded tones, Dansk tried to tell Ben what the trouble was.

The camp may have had its open trial, he said, and heard the U.S. Government judge lay into the stranglers and read not guilty over the head of Ruel Oakes and even to have listened to His Honor pass down sentence of death on Selman Draco for murdering the dancehall tart who had threatened to expose him as father to her unborn child.

But all of this, the smith continued, would thin out in coming daylight. That was what the townfolk feared. Draco would be gone and the judge would be gone, but the stranglers would still be there.

"You cannot blame the people," Dansk concluded. "They know themselves. More, they know you, friend Allison."

147

He went on to say that many in the camp blamed Ben for the deaths of August Wendler, Thomas Clarke, Edward Dobbs, and Charles Farwood, through his original rescue of Ruel Oakes from the Canyon Creek posse. He, Ben, must remember that, no matter what, the mulatto boy was still a speckled nigger to the rough miners of the camp. Judge Handelmann's fine words did not change that. Nor the fact that a white woman had died with a black man's ax in her head. It had nothing to do with justice. It was the way men thought. If Ben could not accept that, let him think of what Dr. Hankins had prescribed for him.

Ben frowned, nodding.

Earlier, the physician had been brought over fairly sober from the Oriental Bar to tend Ben's head wound and the ugly ribcage contusion. He had pronounced the muscular Texan fit for the road, scribbled a prescription for him, torn it off the pad, and departed in some haste back across the street to catch up on his own serious medication.

Advised the urgent scrawl:

> Rx
> Complete change of climate.
> Take first dose tonight . . .
>   sgnd.
> R. J. Hankins, M.D.

It was at this point in the preparations for a daybreak departure that Doud Harriman came in through the rear of the house, plainly concerned not to be seen by those still out in front. When Ben and Dansk came in for another load of Texas goods, he got the former at once aside. He had dark news: "Don't wait for tomorrow, Allison," he warned Ben. "By then it will be spread to every camp south of Virginia and Bannack. It will be all over this camp within another hour tonight. That's the time you've got."

"For what, for God's sake?" Ben demanded.

"Just now," Harriman answered, "Frenchy Burloign

came in from the Bozeman Road, his horse green-lathered."

"What? I thought he was ramrodding the guards taking Draco up to Bozeman."

"He was. Reedler and the Virginia Committee hit them six miles out. Took Draco and rode out."

"Oh, Jesus."

Yes, editor Harriman sympathized, oh, Jesus, for sure.

But let Ben and the others make no mistake. What he and Ruel Oakes had done had struck the stranglers a body blow. They had proved that by their need to take Draco away from the law, but time would be required for the full effect of the mulatto boy's case to come to bear on the consciousness of the rough men along the mining creeks. Meanwhile, when it now became known in Canyon Creek that the vigilantes were still giving blue tickets at midnight, yet were square against open, fair court judgments, it was not likely the citizens would rise up to shelter Ben and Ruel.

"They will cleave to the stranglers," Harriman finished. "Were I you, Allison, I would be in Wyoming come sunrise—not sleeping here, not waiting for the magpies."

"God knows," Ben said, "I thank you."

"You have paid your way, Ben Allison. The thanks are mine and those of this camp and of every camp. Just don't wait for your reward. I will get these stragglers out of the smithy by buying two rounds at the Oriental. Good luck and don't look back."

Ben could see it then clear as the bottom sand of the Rio Concho in late July. Of a sudden he was bellysick of Montana, homesick for Texas and the Kwahadi country and for the Ranger law that rode open in the daylight.

"Friend editor," he said, putting out his hand. "You are four-square and a man whose tongue don't wobble. If you are ever in San Saba, ask for Ben Allison. You will get as good as you have give."

Harriman took his hand and the two men gripped hard. He was gone then and Dansk Jensen had come back in and Ben told him to lock up and turn out the lamps; things had turned tight and would likely squeeze up even more so.

"What is it, friend Ben?"

"The Virginia Committee have took Draco." He looked around with belated alarm. "Where the hell's the kid? And the woman? You seed them?"

"The boy took your Indian horse and left some time ago. He asked that I not tell you. He promised me he would be back soon."

"Jesus, I don't believe it. Old Ruel run out?"

"The lady, too," Jensen said. "But she left a note." He fished in his pocket, found the scrap of paper, gave it over to Ben. "It's good news, ya?" he said hopefully.

Ben scowled his way through the penciled adieu.

"No," he said, "it's good-bye. Ain't even signed."

"Funny thing, ya," frowned the blacksmith. "She was crying pretty good, I think."

"Oh, Christ," Ben groaned. "You any idee, atall, where she might be at?"

"Oh, ya, sure," Dansk brightened. "Come on."

He led the way back out through the smithy and to its lean-to wagon shed where the Murphy stood parked, taking down the smithy lanterns and snuffing them out on the way. They came into the wagon shed, blinking to see.

"Ya," called Dansk Jensen. "You still there, lady?"

"I think it's me," a small voice answered uncertainly. "Make a light and we'll see."

Jensen relit one of the lamps, a bull's-eye shaded model, adjusting the beam to its smallest aperture. The ray fell on Ellie Semple at the wagon's tailgate, busied when they arrived adding her own traveling wardrobe to the supplies already in the Murphy. "Some of my wife's good things," the blacksmith explained lamely to Ben. "What use are they to an old Danish horseshoer?"

Ben, trying to deny the leap his heart gave when he heard Ellie Semple's voice, twisted up his Indian face.

150

"You giving her our damn wagon, too?" he said acridly.

"No, no, the wagon is for all of us."

"*All?*" The dark face contorted yet more. "Of *us?*"

Ellie Semple whacked small hands to not small hips, and struck a pose of eternal female defiance.

"You're getting a heap better, cowboy," she declared. "You are handling those two- and three-letter words just as good as if you knew what they meant. Or could spell them right off."

She did not fool Ben. He could see her nose was yet red from blowing, her green eyes blurry with tears.

"Missus," he said plaintively. "Would you mind telling a poor, out-of-work, part-Injun traildriver from Texas just what the hell you think you are doing pitching your duds up into that-there Murphy wagon?"

"I will leave it to Mr. Jensen!" sniffed Ellie Semple righteously. "I have my packing to attend to."

The blacksmith, pressed for the promised explanation, was doing a lot of stammering and backing away when he was rescued by the sound of a burdened horse approaching up the rear alleyway. Ben snapped out, "Hood the lamp!" He slid out the Colt .44. "Lay back along the wall, both of you. They ain't stopping us now."

But the door did not smash open to a drive of booted vigilante foot. There was no dreaded challenge to hold! Stand fast! Instead, the door creaked open to admit a missing stray, leading a trailworn Comanche gelding so heavily backloaded with six ore-sacks rigged in pairs, pannier-style, wither to tailroot, that he was grunting like a twenty-three-year-old Paiute packmare.

"Psst! Whar at is everybody?" inquired Ruel Oakes. "Lookit hyar what I done brung to he'p start us our new homeplace in Texas."

Ben holstered the .44 with a homeplace oath.

He collared the mulatto youth and dragged him into the wagon shed, hauling Poo Cat in with him and with a separate curse in pure Kwahadi for the Indian pony.

"I'd ought to hide you raw," he told the youth.

"Where in God's name you been? Out collecting stove coal for the starving Absoroky Injuns?"

"No sir, it ain't coal," apologized Ruel.

"Maybe a load of horseshoes," guessed Dansk Jensen, lifting one of the bags. "Ya, heavy as bullet lead!"

"Heavier," said Ruel Oakes. "It's every ounce of it highgrade. Gonner assay anyways twelve, thirteen dollars. That's a ounce, not a pound. And them sacks will run a hard grunt over fifty pound, each one of them." He looked up at the tall man from Texas. "Whoo-ee, Mr. Ben," he said gratefully. "We is nigger rich."

Ben flashed the beam of the bull's-eye lantern into one of the sacks. The raw ore blazed like a lit fire.

"Mr. Ruel," he answered. "*You're* nigger rich; the rest of us are still just poor white trash." He stared on at the dazzle of the gold. "God almighty, boy," he said, "do you know you got to have pushing sixty thousand dollars, Yankee cash, in them old rotted sacks?"

The mulatto boy laughed softly.

"Got to have," he said. "I done thieved it off poor Mr. Pegleg whiles living in the drift with him. Kept having phantom dreams abouten the big stope—knowed it were going to cave. The hants told me to hide up some."

"*Some!*" Ben said. "I would hate to see what a rich nigger would call a fair helping. Whoo-ee, is right."

A voice of female asperity injected itself to cool the rising fever of the gold.

"You two better stop whooeeing and start unloading that poor little horse," Ellie Semple directed. "Providing, that is, you intend accompanying blacksmith Jensen and myself to the Texas country. We are due to leave promptly, come morning."

"Wrong again," Ben said. "You got ten minutes, missus, to get anything else you want out of the house."

"What's the matter?" asked Ruel Oakes, the old fear suddenly back in him. "I thought we was free."

"We are," Ben said, "iffen we hurry."

"It's *them* again," Ruel whispered.

"As ever was," the tall cowboy rasped. "Start dragging sacks."

32

When, scant minutes later, the winter-tight Murphy wagon of blacksmith Jensen wheeled out of the darkened smithy lean-to and off south down Main toward the Canyon Creek Fork, editor Harriman's second round of free drinks had just been poured at the Oriental. The muddy street was bare of traffic, horse or human. It was then sometime after 8:00 P.M. The big Dane, driving, clucked to his matched heavy sorrels, and ticked them lovingly with the light buggywhip. The brawny animals squatted, hit into their collars, made the tugs sing. The Murphy took speed, running silently on fresh-tallowed hubs.

At the tailgate, paired again by fate, Poo Cat and Jensen's stout bay saddler trotted along like the old friends they were becoming. If the Comanche mustang was in equine fact beguiling the stolid Montana gelding with tales of Texas and the sun-blessed Llana Estacado, no human ear could know. But, inside the sturdy Murphy, it took no gift of translation to understand the discourse.

It was pure Ben Allison booster talk of the wonders of the Big Thicket and the Caprock and the Cross Timbers and all of the great cow and buffalo country to the west of his San Saba home, clear on out to the Pecos and the sunset side of the Comanche pastures. To hear him tell it, Ellie Semple would have to guess that all that Ruel Oakes' gold was just so much excess

153

freight. Old Ben would soon enough own Texas with or without the ore sacks of his mulatto business partner. For her part, the one-time woman of the camps was content to lie close and listen. This Indian-dark, bow-legged and soft-drawling tall man from Texas was a new kind to her. He made a woman feel clean and new and like as though that place they were heading for would welcome Ellie June Semple in a way to say she could be whatever Ben said she was. And, as to that, the things he was then saying into her nearest small pink ear were enough to make China Polly blush.

But, God, what matter that?

Good Dansk Jensen was on the driver's seat, the boy Ruel Oakes beside him watching the night and the way of the wagon road past the Bozeman cutoff on into the Canyon Creek Pass Road and, well, a woman was entitled to let down and listen a little. There would soon be a midnight-rest halting at Shafter's Store, through the canyon, getting warmed and fully fed and going on through the starlit night to the Wyoming line by break of day.

That would be some sunrise.

Its light would shine all the way from Sheridan to Red River. Ben had told her if they stood on tiptoe they might see clean to Abilene. And leastways past Casper to Cheyenne. And, why hell, from there it was only Colorado and the Panhandle of Oklahoma stood between them and Texas. "We'll beat April to Amaril-lo," Ben had said, and Ellie sighed and believed him and slept on his arm sweet and light as a child.

There was a halt before Shafter's, but Ellie Semple never knew it.

Ruel kept his soft voice low when he alerted Ben back through the puckerhole in the canvas top of the Murphy wagon, and Dansk Jensen slowed the sorrel team with such careful skill that no rim-iron squealed and no stone broke to awaken the green-eyed sleeper.

Ben eased away from her, out over the tailgate, *hoh-shuhing* the horses, checking the Colt .44 in its leather.

154

"Stay on the seat," he said tersely to Ruel Oakes. "Come on, blacksmith."

He and Dansk Jensen went forward afoot and not talking. They had been there before, and not long before. It had been nighttime then, too, but with no moon. Now the thin cold sliver of the new quarter had arisen and its wan light made the flat more ghostly and unreal and fearsome than when lit with the torches of the stranglers.

The wind still prowled, however, as it had that other time. It stirred the frozen body, squeaking the rope where its cinching bit into the limb of the gnarled tree. Both men came reluctantly up to the corpse. Dansk Jensen had to reach forth and steady it in its turning on the wind and the twist of the rope. "Is it him?" Ben said.

"Ya, sure. Maybe one hour, I think."

They stood there mute in the presence of all that had been mortal of Selman Draco.

"Maybe," said Dansk Jensen, "this will be the last one." He looked at the rope, and then hefted the ax he carried.

"Mebbe," Ben answered.

"Shall I cut him down?" the blacksmith asked.

"No," Ben said quickly. "Go get our horses. Tell the kid to drive on slow, we'll catch up."

Jensen got the horses and they stood with them until Ruel had the wagon moved on across the flat into the south-bending of the canyon for Shafter's Store. When they could no longer hear a creak of wheel nor the breathing of the team, Ben shook out his Texas rope. Seeing him do so, Dansk Jensen understood and uncoiled his own lariat. They got good catches on the old tree's bare limbs. It took five tries, but on the fifth one, both horses driving, they pulled over the sycamore.

The blacksmith chopped the snaggled arms of the hanging tree, using great swinging blows. Ben gathered the limbs, arranged them about the trunk and hollowed stump, making a pyre. In this, he placed the body of Selman Draco. Dansk nodded, understanding now.

155

"An Indian thing, ya?" he said.

Ben nodded in return and struck the match.

They waited until the limbs caught and the long-dead heart of the patriarch broke flame. For many winters only the bark had carried life in the old tree and its stem and limbs, bone-dry, now flared and boomed in showering sparks to the suddenly rising wind.

Ben made a sign into the night and spoke a single word in guttural Comanche, *"Nanewawke,"* and made for the waiting Poo Cat. Jensen followed him, swinging up on the bay. "It was a good word?" he said. "Yes," Ben said, checking the mustang. "It means he paid for his damages in this world."

They held a last moment, and Dansk Jensen added softly, "Ya, and maybe one other thing—maybe no more for the sycamore."

Ben Allison did not answer.

Together, he and the blacksmith sent their horses on the lope after the Murphy wagon.

After they had gone, a coyote trotted out of the brush and through the scattered boulders. It was a dog coyote, old to that country and to the sandy flat called gallows tree. The animal stared at the burning pyre, dying back now, and whined anxiously. The limbs, settling, fell inward with a crash of embers, frightening the old coyote. He circled away, up the slope, without looking back.

Something was not as it had been down there.

Something had changed.

It disturbed the old fellow. He tucked tail, elevated his graying muzzle, and howled dolefully. When he went away in a little while, he came not again to gallows tree flat, nor did the Vigilantes of Montana.

Something *had* changed.

As for the outcasts of Canyon Creek and big Ben Allison, they knew nothing whatever of Montana beyond that final night, nor cared. It is said that, once safely away into Wyoming, they laughed all the way to Texas and the Rio Grande. Well, at least to Red River. Or was it to April in Amarillo?

156

No matter, *amigos:* Who would know of such things in Montana?

But if you are ever in San Saba and ask for Ben Allison, ah! that's another Indian pony altogether. They will tell you the simple truth about him and you may depend on it absolutely.

He was a very tall man.

BEYOND
THE GALLOWS TREE

Some biographical footnotes
on Ben K. Allison and the
Montana Stranglers

There are forever small veins and pockets left un-mined after the main streak runs out. So with the matter of Ben Allison and the gold-strike camp of Canyon Creek, Montana. When the sometime road agent, gunfighter, trailherd drover, and Confederate Cavalry raider went home to Texas that long-ago win-ter night, the accounts were not quite tidied.

As to the murder charge which originally earned the San Saba cowboy his blue ticket from the Virginia Committee—the robbery-death of J. C. Marriot on the isolated Bozeman Wagon Road—Selman Draco report-edly confessed the crime to F. X. Reedler and the "Virginia Ten" when finally faced with the rope. Con-cerning the ten thousand dollars missing in the brutal case, the Executive is reputed to have replied, "The funds were urgently required in a matter of personal honor and of extreme import to the work." It was said in the community that the import had to do with the pregnancy of the Vardeen girl, who was allegedly threatening the Executive with exposure unless he came up with the money to "make things lastingly right for me and the baby."

Coming to a history on Billie Dove, her working associate Mrs. Elvira J. Semple, under skilled interro-gation by lawyer Esau Lazarus, testified on the day of the miners' court that the so-called poor Vardeen creature was anything but the innocent dove she feigned to be. She was indeed no kind of a bird to be pitied. Censored would be the more accurate term for Miss Billie Dove. She had, according to the Semple testimony, worked the same "knocked-up" routine on no less than five other prominent citizens in as many other mining camps, Colorado to California, yet was but nineteen years of age in her farewell performance with Selman Draco. In this case she was indeed with child, but the probable sire, as established by Lazarus, was a young faro dealer of the lawyer's acquaintance, last employed in Nathan Stark's Black Nugget Saloon in Virginia City.

In his appearance before the sixteen-man miners' court jury, Walter J. Gates, if a yellowed newsclip under the byline of Doud Harriman in the Canyon City *Crier* is to be accepted as documentation, brought into the Masonic Hall his entire theatrical accoutrements and, "before the very eyes of his astounded rough audience, the members of which had surely never viewed such marvels heretofore," transformed himself from Pegleg Gates to Fagan Ratsmith, "all in the time of twenty good drags upon a Habana cheroot."

The old man did not linger to savor his triumphal return. Within a fortnight after blacksmith Jensen willed him his decent small house next the Blue Light Livery Barn, Pegleg was "gone again."

He is said to have been seen subsequently in every major strike from Idaho Bar to Dinky Creek to Dawson and Nome. And to have died, finally, at age one hundred and three years in the Pioneer Home at Fairbanks, Alaska, sometime in the spring of 1925. One thing remains certain; the only reason the old rascal hung about Canyon Creek the two weeks that he did was to mine by night the three known entrances to his vast mine—those of Old Cabin, Main Drift, and Little Canyon Creek. When the charges went off simultaneously in the middle of that spectacular "last night" they not only blew cabin, drift, and creek entrances but took off the face of the ridge and the body of the ore-dump, spreading them over half of Canyon Creek

County. The old shack was literally obliterated, the creek's course altered to run outside the mountain in a new channel, or, as some snooty geologists from the state university later explained, "to run again in its original streambed from whence it had been forced by earth violence centuries gone to flow through the honeycombed monolith." It was this same night that Walter J. "Pegleg" Gates disappeared once more, never hence to be seen alive in Canyon Creek. There were naturally those who insisted that "the old idiot has blowed hisse'f up agin," but they were the same ones who had known for certain that he had died in the mountain those older years gone, when his ghost prowled the Old Glory until so happily laid to rest by young Ruel Oakes.

In result of the incredible success of Pegleg's last sapping of Ghost Ridge—sometimes called Ghost Hill—all traces of the true entrances to the Old Glory faded beneath the snows and new forest growth of the decades. By 1900, the Old Glory was already an accepted ghost mine. Today, it is sought in Montana with the same fervor that Arizonans lavish upon the Lost Dutchman and the Lost Adams Diggings. Or that Chihuahuans and Sonorans devote to following "genuine Jesuit maps" to the buried portals of the Lost Tayopa Mine. "The Lost Ridge," "Ghost Hill Glory Hole," "Ghost Stope," "Golden Gopher Mine," and "The Lost Creek Bonanza" are but a few of the names still muttered by very old men with watery eyes and bent spines leading equally old jack burros through a dozen outcrop flanks, spurs, and assorted other small mountain children of the main Rockies looking for Pegleg's fabled gold stope. But it is difficult enough to locate a guide who can even show the curious where Canyon Creek itself once grew its canvas saloons and bucksawed green pine shacks, much less, in these latter cynical times, to find one who can take the questioner to the "very ridge" where Pegleg made his discovery strike. One has to believe that old Walter Gates is still giggling hee hee hee! somewhere up in that last great glory hole in the Big Sky.

The vigilante movement, already under some public pressure in those later years of the Canyon Creek find, was no doubt "helped" out of popular favor by the rash one-man intervention of Texan Ben K. Allison in the matter of the summary execution of the runaway slave boy, Ruel Oakes. The hanging of Selman Draco at gallows tree flat was indeed the final such "decision" attributed to the once all-powerful Committee—and it was never acknowledged by either Nathan Stark or F. X. Reedler, the claims of editor Harriman and the Canyon Creek *Crier* notwithstanding.

Harriman, incidentally, never actually repudiated the vigilante movement of which he was, of course, a founding member. His criticism of the system of what Thomas Dimsdale has called "popular justice in the Rocky Mountains" was restricted to the particular weakness inherent in it whereby a Selman Draco could "wickedly and horribly" pervert the original high purposes of the Vigilance Committee. Harriman later removed to the San Francisco area where he became a reporter for the old *Chronicle* and wrote a successful book on the roots and reputations of the vigilante movement of 1849–51–56, climaxing in the repugnant and brutal murder of James King, editor of the *Daily Evening Bulletin*.

Nathan Stark also "went West" to California. He became enormously wealthy in land, cattle, mines and railroading, served to the end, and some say to the entire result of his success, by the faithful hand and brilliant mind of Esau Lazarus.

The Texas leads are less distinct.

It is known that Ruel Oakes lived both with the Comanche kin of Ben Allison and with the Danish blacksmith Dansk Jensen who, for twenty years, kept a widely known smithy on Sabido Creek, near San Saba. Jensen put the mulatto boy through school, adopted him legally, treated him in every way as an own son. Ruel studied law and in later years settled in the Cherokee Strip where he had a lucrative practice in chattel property cases, mainly of cattlemen in range dispute. He married a Cherokee girl by whom he had eleven children. The firstborn, Ben Allison Oakes, was the wealthiest "red rancher" in Oklahoma and was nearly elected U.S. Senator from there. Several of the other Oakes boys were outstanding citizens and three of the girls married rich and influential white Oklahomans. Ruel, it might fairly be said, found his freedom with a vengeance. And just possibly funded it with something heavier and more negotiable than the windy promises of equality through black emancipation.

Elvira Semple went the other way. Convinced by a bit of life with Ben "out on the wild San Saba," that cows and cowboys and crazy-riding Comanche kinfolk did not comprise her entire vision of the higher grail, Ellie opened a house of, well, not notably hale repute, in the middle of downtown Dallas. Her founding customers were the millionaire cattlemen in from Fort Worth, and the later oil moguls from the East Texas fields. Ellie, like Ruel Oakes, "made it pay."

Ben Allison is harder to track. The tall Texan, never a communicative man, left nothing of written nature about himself or the remarkable adventures of his life. Some say Ben was simply illiterate and could not write. Others maintain testily that he could for damned certain make his mark with something longer than an X, that he did not, goddamnit, read his newspapers upside down, and that Old Ben had "chose deliberate a'purpose to leave it lay where it scattered, insofar as any hand-wrote rememories of him, or his, was concerned." That sounds like Ben and this biographer happily accepts it. The storehouse of his life but grows the richer for lack of binding memoir. The folklores of the land survive its records. As the salty old boys tilted in their rickety chairs at the livery barn any Saturday afternoon in San Saba will tell you, "What the hell is facts, anyways, but a pack of damned lied settled on?"

Among the most trusted keepers of Ben Allison *fabulas* are the *mestizos,* the Indian and Mexican mixed-bloods of the Chihuahuan Sierra Madre. It is they who, in the present matter, will glance carefully about, and say, *"Escuchan, muchachos;* listen to this:"

In the same spring that "big Benito" came home to

163

Hawk Shadow Ranch from far *Montaña,* the small son of the Governor of Texas was stolen by Mexican Apaches raiding up out of Chihuahua State. It was assumed the boy was lost, his capture a cruel accident of frontier chance, his fate assured by the fates of white children stolen before him. It was not so. After many weeks a ransom note appeared demanding an incredible, an unthinkable thing; the surrender, in exchange for the boy's life, of all small arms and ammunitions in the arsenal at Fort Bliss, Post of El Paso.

> ". . . every rifle, every round,
> each *pistola,* pound of powder,
> cap, ball, bulletmold, patch
> and ramming-rod under roof . . .
> all without betrayals, or the
> boys dies for the treachery . . ."

The note was in English, white man's words, almost certainly. *De seguro,* it was not the work of an Indian or Mexican. Yet it did say the boy was held in dreaded Pa-gotzin-kay, the Apache's Sierra Madre fortress. And the note's bearer was a Mexican of Casas Grandes, in Chihuahua, storied portal into the high ranges rearing between that state and Sonora wherein, the legend said, lay the grim Apache stronghold.

There were added terse admonishments:

A solitary messenger must come from the governor. He must bring acceptance of terms, bear authority to arrange exchanges. If other than a single man were sent, all was done. There must be no public knowledge, anywhere. Such leakage would kill the boy as certainly as other failures.

There was no signature, no date, nothing else.

Yes, Patron, it was understood that the messenger must go to Pa-gotzin-kay. But, alas, *hay historia otra del todo.* That is another story altogether. Do not seek to ask if big Benito were indeed the man of the Governor, the one chosen to go. This cannot be revealed. Forgive it, but who knows what spirits of the past ride out by night on Apache horses from the burial caves at Pa-gotzin-kay? Let it rest, Patron, *por favor*. Still, you have been respectful, attentive. One appreciates that in these days. A single thing may be hinted, but treat it as a trust of brothers, a confidence of the *monte*.

If you are *Tejano* and wish truly to learn if the Tall One found Pa-gotzin-kay, if he saved the small son of the governor of Texas, ask it then of your own *Americano* Apaches. Let them tell you. We do not fear them. They are *gringo* Indians. They do not come to ride at night above the ground in Old Chihuahua. But, *mas cuidado, hombre,* all the same.

Who really knows about these ancient things?

RELAX!
SIT DOWN
and Catch Up On Your Reading!